White Harbor Road

and Other Tales of Paranormal Romance

by
Evelyn Klebert

White Harbor Road
and Other Tales of Paranormal Romance
By Evelyn Klebert

A Cornerstone Book
Published by Cornerstone Book Publishers

Copyright © 2012 & 2024 by Evelyn Klebert

First Cornerstone Edition - 2012
Second Cornerstone Edition – 2024

Cornerstone Book Publishers
Hot Springs Village, AR
www.cornerstonepublishers.com

ISBN: 978-1-61342-066-9

Dedication

For Those Who Have Moved On
Whose Example still Guides Us

Table of Contents

White Harbor Road 1

What is Circumspect? by Sophie Wilde 43

A Few Moments with a Stranger 70

The Lake 82

The Most Unlikely of Places.........................98

White Harbor Road

I t wasn't exactly as she'd intended, but the truth was that nothing ever was exactly as she intended. It was Christmas, the Christmas holidays, and she had three weeks off teaching at the University. But she wouldn't be traveling home. Her parents were off to visit her sister's family in North Carolina — a trip she simply couldn't face. So, instead, Helen had decided to do something odd and spontaneous that no one really understood. She'd decided to rent a beach cottage and spend Christmas alone.

"You can't spend the holidays alone, dear."

"That's just odd."

And a maelstrom of other responses, but she was thirty-six years old, unattached. And her heart craved something indefinable. But as was not unusual, her plans did not turn out as she expected.

"This is not a beachside cottage."

The manager, a woman in her early sixties with abundant white hair, smiled at her broadly, clearly unruffled. "If you follow this street down White Harbor Road, you will hit the beach in no time."

Helen frowned. On the internet, it had advertised a Gulf Coast beachside cottage. "That's not exactly the same as a beachside cottage. I wanted to be near the water."

Mrs. Haughn smiled again with genuine warmth, smoothly, as though utterly untouched by misunderstanding. "You know, Miss Ellis, it is Miss?"

"Lately, it's been Ms."

Another smile, "Ms. Ellis, I would be happy to refund your deposit, but I must tell you I think you're making a mistake. This sweet little cottage is right in the midst of historical Crystal Springs. Just turn a corner, and you're walking down a lovely street filled with shops owned by our artistic residents. And my dear, you can walk to the beach. It's only three, well, maybe four blocks down, a lovely jaunt in this cool weather."

Her head spun a bit. It wasn't what she'd planned. She'd planned to be well isolated, work on the novel she'd been piddling with for the last two years, and listen to the sound of the water, not of cars driving by. "I don't know, Mrs. Haughn. It's just not exactly what I had planned."

"Well, my dear, why don't you try it out for a few days. Plans can change sometimes, change and often for the better."

It was a lovely cottage with wooden floors and a cozy bedroom with a full-size bed covered in a light blue chenille bedspread that reminded her of her grandmother for some odd reason. There was also a tiny sort of den with a comfortable overstuffed chair and a television that she did not intend to use, then a connecting open kitchen with a small dinette table. All in all, it was very comfortable, very solitary, and there was free wireless. It fit the bill for what she wanted, except she wished all of it were sitting right on the beach.

"Helen."

"Hmm?"

"It's not too late to catch a flight to North Carolina. I hate the idea of you spending Christmas alone."

"No, no, don't worry. I need this time to figure some things out."

Actually, Mrs. Haughn was just slightly off. The beach was a five-block walk from the Seaside Cottages. That was even their name — Seaside Cottages. But the first morning, actually a Sunday morning, Helen bundled up and made the jaunt. Living in the South, one would think the winters weren't as cold, but they'd be wrong. There might be an absence of snow, but the moisture in the air made the cold so penetrative. As she walked, Helen pulled the heavy teal-colored scarf wrapped around her neck slightly upward to cover the bottom part of her face.

The beach itself was definitely worth the walk once she arrived. The day was gray and overcast, but the white sand gleamed. The water soothingly lapped up on the shore. She sat on a cold granite bench for a moment placed in a park-like area leading up to the sand. She breathed the cool air into her lungs as she considered for the first time that perhaps she'd made a mistake. Christmas was in four days, and she would be alone. It hadn't bothered her before, not really. She'd felt determined, possessed in some way to be isolated, but now there were doubts — *the best-laid plans.*

She bowed her head, overcome with a sudden surge of confusing despair when out of nowhere, she felt a long, cold nose nudge her. Her head pulled up, and she met the large, dark eyes of a black dog. It aggressively pushed its face into her hands so she would pet it.

Finally, regaining her bearings after being so startled, she noticed the long, slim dog was leashed and followed its long connection to a man standing quietly a few feet away. "Don't worry. She's harmless," he commented. Helen slowly stood up, though the dog was still intent on nuzzling her. "You know, she doesn't take to everyone but seems to like you."

He was tall, tall with a big blue jacket on. "Well, she's beautiful. I didn't notice you two walk up."

He pressed a button, reeling the leash in a bit tighter as he approached her. "You seemed like you wanted to be alone. I planned to walk by, but then Hazel had other plans."

She laughed, "She's a lab?"

"Lab, collie, a mix of other things."

She smiled, nodding. He was closer now — brown hair, beard, and mustache, maybe forties, she thought. "Are you—" then she stopped.

"Are we—" he echoed in a friendly manner.

"Sorry, I was going to ask if you were from here."

"Ah, Crystal Springs, not originally, but I've lived here for the last three years. It's a lovely little antiquated community. And I would say quite definitively that you are not."

She laughed nervously, "No, I guess that's obvious."

"Yes, but not for the reasons you may think. Visiting?"

She nodded, "Yes, I rented a cottage."

"Ah, one of Mary Haughn's cottages down White Harbor Road?"

"Yes," she answered, a bit surprised.

"Over Christmas here alone?"

She sighed a bit in response, trying to decide how to respond.

And then he smiled, "Would you like to get a coffee. It's just into town."

Now, that was quick and unexpected, seeing as though they'd literally just met. "I suppose," she answered a bit hesitantly. "I'm sorry. I didn't get your name."

"No, you didn't. My name is Billy Struve."

"Nice to meet you. I'm Helen, Helen Ellis."

It was a small café/coffee shop just off Main Street. And by the time they arrived, she was grateful. She'd thought she was in good shape, but all the walking this morning had proved differently. Mr. Billy Struve had tied Hazel to the white wrought iron chair across from hers on the café's patio, asking her to keep watch as he disappe into the restaurant. The patio was positioned just off the street, where she could observe people milling around, wandering from shop to shop. It was actually quite soothing, a different pace from the city where these days nothing much felt languid.

In moments, she was pulled from her thoughts back to the presence of her companion, arriving with two steaming cups of coffee and two almond croissants. He smiled, sitting across from her. "I hope you don't mind. I thought you might be hungry. Breakfast went right by me today."

Strangely, she hadn't given a thought to breakfast this morning. She had just focused on the necessity of getting out by the water. "Oh, actually, it's perfect, thank you," she answered.

She hadn't looked too closely at her companion on their jaunt here. There was some conversation, but purely superficial, about the lovely houses near the water, the weather, the beautiful day, and Hazel. She learned quickly all there was to know about Hazel — an SPCA dog he'd adopted as a puppy just after he'd moved here. He took a sip of his coffee and more than a few bites of his croissant and leaned back in his chair, eying her amiably. "So, you work here?" she asked a little awkwardly.

"Yes, I own one of the shops in the area. It's a bit of a gallery for painters, sculptors, and other artists."

"Oh, that's interesting. What about you? Are you an artist?" It was an odd question that had simply popped into her head. But he seemed to take it in his stride as though he was not surprised.

"Yes, Helen, as a matter of fact, I am a painter and make pottery as well."

She nodded, "So you sell?"

"My work, as well as others," he answered fluidly, completing her thought. "And you are a writer?" he asked as he sipped his coffee.

The question hit her strangely. "No, not really. Why would you say that?"

He hesitated, almost as though he didn't believe her, then shrugged, "Felt right."

She glanced away, feeling a little uncomfortable now. "I'm a professor in New Orleans. I teach English."

He slowly lowered his coffee cup to the table. "Hmm, strange, you just have that writer vibe, you know."

She turned back to him and added, "I guess I dabbled in it a bit, my own writing."

"Well, Helen Ellis, I have a sense of these sort of things, and I think you should do more than dabble. You should commit to it. I'm sure you'd be wonderful."

She felt a bit stunned at his pronouncement, at how personal he was getting. "And this you know from our short acquaintance?"

"Hmm, don't mean for you to get your back up. In my experience, it's important to do what your soul craves." And then he smiled warmly, "If you don't, it won't give you any peace. You see, I was a lawyer and practiced in Georgia for many years. Then I gave it all up and came here."

"Really?" she asked, a bit surprised.

"Seems reckless, I suppose to some. But I don't think you can put too high a premium on peace." She felt stunned, having no idea at all what to say. "So Helen, since we're being candid, is there anything else you'd like to know?"

"What do you mean?"

"Well, I'm not married, have been, have been divorced, have no children."

She nodded, not at all sure where he was going with this. "Oh, well, that's nice."

He laughed, "Yes, my point is that if we're finished with me now, I would like to know about you. Why has such a lovely woman come to this place, a place she clearly doesn't know, alone for the holidays? Why?" and then he smiled in that warm way of his, "And why again?"

She sipped her coffee, wondering if it was time to leave and start closing doors. "It's not a mystery. I wanted to get away, alone. That's all."

"And write?" he asked.

"Maybe," she hesitated.

"Been married, Helen?"

Another odd moment in a series of odd moments since she'd met this man. "Yes, once, a while ago," she answered with a distance in her voice.

He nodded slowly as though it was of no surprise. "Thought so."

"Why, why would you think so?"

And then he looked past her to the people milling on the sidewalks, "Because these things leave marks."

After coffee, they walked around Main Street, Billy Struve amiably pointing out this establishment and then the next. She found herself drifting into a peaceful zone, one that was not contemplating her next move or analyzing the implications of what was happening. She was simply moving in the moment, a soothing place to exist.

"Are you getting tired?" he asked.

"I don't know. Maybe a bit. I'm not really used to walking this much."

"Well, we don't want to wear you out on your first day. How about I walk you home?"

"All right," she answered as he changed directions, following his moderate strides back towards White Harbor Road.

"You know, I was thinking Helen Ellis. Why don't you let me fix you dinner tonight?"

She breathed in the frosty air, her city upbringing creeping back into her mind with doubts. After all, Billy Struve was a virtual stranger. What did she really know about him, except that he was pleasant, laid-back, and —

"Only the things he has told you he is."

She halted in the middle of the road at his strange pronouncement mirroring her thoughts. "What did you say?" she asked.

He frowned, "Sorry, I told you I get a sense of things. You're worried about whether you can really trust me."

"How did you know what I was thinking?"

"Helen, it's not such an incredible jump to make. Tell you what. I'll take you out to dinner in Biloxi. Things roll up early here in this sleepy little town. Would that be better?"

She started walking again but slowly, a bit taken aback by what had just happened. "I don't know."

"Hmm, look, I like spending time with you. You seem, how can I say this, kindred to me. So, don't overthink it, all right."

She didn't answer. She just let his pronouncement float solitarily in the air as they turned another corner into the parking lot of Mary Haughn's cottages.

"So, how's the great experiment going?"

"Fine, it's beautiful here."

"You know, we could still get you a last-minute ticket to fly up here for Christmas," Helen could hear a bit of strain in Lydia's usually cheerful voice. Evidently, her mother had pressured her to make this scenario happen.

"Thanks, but I'm all set up here. And I think it's doing me some good."

"Oh, okay, met anybody interesting?"

She sighed, questioning whether to open this up, but in truth, it would be reassuring to them to know she wasn't completely alone. "Actually, yes, I met a man on the beach this morning, and we're having dinner tonight."

Helen dressed in one of the few slightly dressy outfits she'd brought — a dark green wool skirt and matching sweater with boots, her favorite cold-weather accessory. Just after six, she heard the quick light knock at her cottage door. She'd spent most of the afternoon resting and then actually for the remaining hour or two writing. She was gratified at finally getting some of this work done. The normal distractions that always seemed to vex her were absent here. Truly, it was as though she'd escaped, at least temporarily, to a different reality.

"You look beautiful," he immediately commented as Billy Struve crossed the threshold into her small den.

"Oh, thanks," she responded. He was so gracious and smoothly attentive that it surprised her. Most people orbiting her sphere of contacts lately seemed more self-absorbed, completely focused on keeping their personal realm intact. As a result, giving wasn't a high priority.

He was dressed nicely, too, wearing a sweater over dress pants and a long trench coat that gave him a different, sharper look, as though she could now imagine him as the lawyer he had claimed to be.

"Look, I'm sorry about brushing you off, I mean about dinner at your house."

"No, don't give it a second thought, too soon. That's my problem. Once I set my mind to something, I'm ready to move ahead full steam."

She picked up her long gray coat, and he immediately took hold of it, helping her into it. "Set your mind to what exactly?"

He grinned a bit, "Yeah, hmm, how about seafood? I know a good restaurant."

"Sounds fine," she said, realizing he would not answer.

It was dusk, and they traveled the long, quiet stretch of beach road into Biloxi. Billy Struve drove a Jeep Cherokee that was filled with various extraneous equipment in the back denoting a more rural existence than she was used to. It was strange. The pace here seemed more mellow and calmer, but the further they traveled away from Crystal Springs, that feeling of tranquility seemed to dissipate.

"You feel it?" he murmured.

She turned to him with curiosity. Their conversation had died off since he'd initially picked her up at the cottage. In fact, so gradually that she hadn't even acknowledged it. "Feel it?" she asked.

"The change," he said.

She smiled. He certainly was being opaque. "I'm sorry. Maybe I'm a bit thick, but I don't follow."

He shook his head, his eyes still fixed on the long curving stretch of beachside road. "I just mean the feeling. It changes once you get out of Crystal Springs. Of course, it's lovely here along the water, but there is something particular and special about that little town. That's why I originally suggested cooking you dinner, all decorum aside. I thought you weren't ready to leave yet."

"Ready to leave?" she echoed with some confusion.

He sighed, "Sorry, I mean, never mind. Here we are," he noted, as she looked up, seeing the corporal limits sign for Biloxi.

Helen Ellis was a blond, a blond with rather large hazel eyes. And he had to admit, she was beautiful. All these facts sort of hit him like a rock in the side of the head. They'd settled into their table at The Seagull, a nice table where they could see the water, even though the light of the day was nearly gone. The waves felt a bit more turbulent tonight, just a bit, by degrees. Perhaps there was a storm coming, but none was forecast. Then again, possibly, he was projecting his own somewhat tumultuous thoughts onto the scenery. He'd felt sure that when he came here, that when she came here, he would be prepared. But now, it didn't feel that way, not nearly.

She glanced up from behind the menu, a lovely smile but something else, a pensiveness. "What do you recommend?" she asked lightly.

He breathed in deeply, coaxing patience to himself. He'd tried to refrain as much as possible from canvassing her thoughts. No matter how tempted he was. And he was tempted. Helen wore a veneer, a protective veneer. It wasn't so obvious who she was. One had to dig to find it. On the surface, she appeared to be a smooth, serene pearl, fluid, pleasing, lovely. But beneath, and it was beneath he was interested in, it was a different story. "Well, that all depends on how hungry you are."

She smiled tentatively, "Not really all that hungry."

"Then the redfish or the flounder."

She nodded, closing the menu and putting it softly down in front of her. "So, tell me, Mr. Struve. What did you mean about Crystal Springs and the feeling there?"

He placed his menu down in front of him as well. Tactful buddy, not too much too soon, or she'll scare away. "You know, the Indians originally settled that area. They felt something special there, mystical energy, if you will. It's my experience every place has its own energy. Your city, New Orleans, being so large, is overlaid with many different energy imprints. But this little town, there is something encased about it, strong, pure, consistent. It's healing."

Her eyes had never left his face, those large, deep eyes. "Do you believe all of that?" she asked hesitantly.

"Billy."

"Okay, Billy, do you believe all of that about the city, I mean?"

"Well, there is more than is dreamed of in our philosophy, Horatio."

She'd almost asked him another question, but the waiter arrived just in time. It was better, with small steps and small truths to digest a little at a time.

She'd decided. This was it. She would have this dinner with him, and then the rest of her time in Crystal Springs would be reflective, solitary, and uncomplicated. The man sitting across from her, engaging her in relaxed, entertaining conversation, was anything but uncomplicated. On the surface, he was handsome, in a rugged way, intelligent, thoughtful, and at first glance, easy-going. But this was not her first time around the block, and she had the intense impression that she was being handled.

"How's the fish?" he asked.

She glanced up, pulling herself out of her troubled assessments. "Oh, you were right. It's great."

He hesitated, his eyes on her face, and it disturbed her. All evening, she would catch him doing this, weirdly looking beyond what she'd said. "What's wrong, Helen?" he asked.

That was it, too perceptive. He was too damn perceptive. "Oh, nothing really. I just have a lot on my mind."

Again, with that stare, but the warm bluish eyes simultaneously put her at ease and made her nervous. She worked to steady herself. This wasn't happening. Whatever this was, wasn't happening. "Am I making you nervous?" he said placidly.

She shook her head in reflex. Her mother's influence — never hurt anyone's feelings. Be tactful. "No, no this is all lovely. I just—I'm not sure how to say this."

He frowned, "Well, if you have to be that anxious, it's best just come out and say it."

Directness, refreshing, disarming. "I just don't want to give the wrong impression. I came here, well, to figure some things out quietly. I don't want things to get complicated."

"Friendship." He stated a bit bluntly.

"What?" she answered with confusion.

"I'm just offering friendship. I like you, Helen, and I could use a friend. Is that acceptable?"

She eyed him with confusion. It sounded so, on the surface, perfectly acceptable.

"You know, your abilities are getting stronger, William."

He frowned, "I know. Sometimes, it's difficult to control them. I don't want to see auras bleeding out of everyone as I walk down the street."

"Sometimes, it takes time for natural talents to develop, and, of course, this place is especially conducive to psychic energies." Sara Morgan, the lovely lady he sat across from on the rug in her den, began to cough very lightly and then reached for a cup of tea she'd placed on the coffee table beside them.

"Are you sure you're feeling up to this, Sara?"

She smiled softly. She was a slight silver-haired woman in her late sixties and a bona fide psychic. She'd come to live in Crystal Springs just six months before he'd settled there. She ran a small metaphysical bookstore and gift shop. After a brief acquaintance, he'd begun taking classes from her, first for stress control and then later for other pursuits. "It will pass," she murmured. "Any more dreams?" she asked.

"Yes, several times a week."

"The same woman?"

"Yes, we meet on the beach, and then we talk, talk about everything, and then sometimes just sit there. I can't really see her face, but her energy, I know. It's so familiar."

She nodded, "She's coming, maybe another year," she murmured.

And it had been as Sara had predicted. And unfortunately, six months earlier, his teacher had crossed over, passing away from an affliction she had opted to keep private.

He'd scared her. Too much too soon, that's a lesson that Sara had often stressed that he needed to learn, patience — the ability to allow things to unfold in their own time. They were traveling along the long, dark road back to Crystal Springs. The darkness of the winter night was thick just now, heavy and dense. And her mood reflected it. He could feel that her thoughts were somber, somewhere else. Stuck in some painful rivet from the past, he suspected. "Doing all right?" he asked.

She roused from that gray, misty place where she'd resided only moments before. "Yes, sorry," she said. "It's so dark tonight. Is this the way it usually is around here?"

"At times, seems more so in the winter."

She sighed deeply, "You didn't tell me. Do you have family?"

"I have a brother up North and a sister out West. My parents have passed on."

"And they didn't want you to visit for Christmas?"

"Well, I have to say it didn't really come up. They have their own families, their own lives, and we were never what you would call a close-knit bunch."

She responded pensively. "This is really my first Christmas away from some kind of family. And you'd swear I was stealing the Crown jewels, the way everyone is reacting."

"Good to know they care."

"Hmm, I don't know if it's that or if they are just being shocked I'm not doing what they expect me to do. They don't take to change very well."

"How about you?"

"What?"

"How do you take to change, Helen?"

There was a pause, and he could feel she was actually genuinely considering the question. "I'm not sure. I haven't had very much lately."

It was strange, unexpected. She was comfortable being with Billy Struve and yet not — relaxed and yet tense. She'd decided not to see him again and yet couldn't seem to follow through.

The dinner was nice, and he'd taken her to a coffee shop later. Nothing earth-shattering happened, but it felt as though something had happened—something she couldn't put her finger on. And then he'd taken her home. He talked about his shop off of Main Street and invited her to drop by.

Her response was vague, and he seemed undaunted. A good night at her door, a slight hug, and then he was gone. And she felt, well, clearly not quite herself.

It was after eleven, and the darkness of the cottage wrapped around her. She eased out of the bed and wrapped herself in a soft, fluffy pink robe she'd brought from the city. It was comforting. There had been many sleepless nights like this one when she'd wrapped up in it, settling into the large blue-gray lazy boy she'd taken with her when her marriage had ended.

Here, there was only the large over-stuffed armchair in front of the TV. But it would have to suffice, and she curled up in it, tucking her feet beneath the robe. She'd tried not to think of it much, but she supposed that was when everything changed, at least when she changed. As marriages go, hers was short-lived. Just two years and most family and friends had commented supportively, "Well, at least you didn't invest too much. There were no children, no real entanglements."

At the time, she'd responded numbly to such comments, but in retrospect, she wondered exactly what they could be thinking.

She'd come out of it changed. The sparkle had gone out of things, the enthusiasm from youth, and yes, the innocence. She'd left much on that doorstep, so strange. Kevin wasn't a bad guy by any means. But together, well, it drained something out of her, something she didn't know how to get back.

There was a chill in the air. She supposed she could turn on the heater, but that would take effort, and a perceptible grogginess was slipping in. She let her head rest softly on the back of the chair and closed her eyes, unwilling to make an effort to return to bed.

Hazel was restless when he returned home. She knew as well. She'd taken immediately to Helen Ellis as had he. For a full two years, he'd been aware of her presence. It had slowly seeped into his dreams and then his waking thoughts. At first, it seemed like some sort of fantasy, perhaps like an imaginary friend from his youth. But then, the impressions became more insistent.

And tonight, the pull was strong, maybe because they'd finally met in the flesh. But her flesh, her free will, was resisting this, even though her spirit felt differently. He heard the rush of wind chimes just outside the French doors in his bedroom which led onto a secluded patio. Patting Hazel lightly on the head, he gently put her out of the room and then pulled on his jacket. As he opened the doors, he could make out shadows, but he reached for the lights on the wall to light up the stone patio.

It startled him at first, the figure he saw down the steps moving across the granite stone pattern he'd designed himself. She was dressed in a long white nightgown, just silently wandering barefoot across the patio. It was startling to find her here, such a direct contact. But he cleared his mind and directed his thoughts to Helen.

"What do you need?"

The figure stopped and turned to him with no expression on her face. It was her and not her — a spiritual manifestation, reaching out, feeling the powerful connection between them as had he. There was silence in response but also confusion and yearning.

"How we make our own prisons," he murmured. And then she was gone. Shakily, he sat in one of the wrought iron chairs near the matching table. He felt shaky all over. She would seek him out again. He was sure of it. After all, it was what her spirit wanted.

It was her intent to resist, instead, to spend the day writing or perhaps taking another walk on the beach or perhaps even a long ride along the coast. All of these were distinct possibilities. But she had decided against walking into town and heading in the general direction of Billy Struve's place of business. Helen had decided after a somewhat restless night that she would avoid this and him. But of course, just after lunch, after one, her feet were itchy for exploration. And they began to draw her in the direction she had decided against.

"Just friendship" was what he was looking for. That was what he had said. But as had been her experience, what one said was not exactly always what one meant. Kevin, her ex-husband, had said he supported everything she wanted to do and was enamored of all she was. But that was before they were married, before he began to chisel away at her dreams by piece by piece, slowly and methodically, until it almost went unnoticed by her. Of course, upon reflection, she never felt as though he did it deliberately. It was just his nature to absorb what was around him and funnel its energy to benefit himself. She often chastised herself for not being more of a fighter in the relationship and less of a giver. But then again, she had never envisioned a relationship where she would have to fight. It went against her grain.

She drifted toward Main Street and noted how busy it was but with more foot traffic than cars. *"A right off of Main Street onto Pine.*" That was what he had told her. Again, she questioned the wisdom of seeing him again. Would that denote too much interest on her part? But something pulled her, something unconscious. And she disregarded her better instincts. She smiled in appreciation as she turned the corner and spotted his establishment. Artistically scripted across the window was the word *Illuminations*. He hadn't told her the store's name, but she knew it was his. With a deep breath and not another thought, she turned the knob, where she was greeted by the happy bark of Hazel that drifted in from somewhere in the back of the store.

She was initially overwhelmed, actually stunned, by an impressive array of glass shelves decorated by all manner of artistry imaginable. She simply stopped in the middle of the significantly large room, allowing her eyes to travel and soak in all that was around her — pottery, jewelry, paintings, baskets, all manner of decorative items formed from seashells. And it felt, it felt as though light and energy poured through the room, so much that it was dizzying. "What do you think?" His voice took her by surprise, but she was more surprised by the fact that he was right beside her, evidently moving next to her while she was completely distracted by what she was seeing.

She turned to him a bit shakily, "You startled me."

He smiled, his face more pensive now as though he was a bit preoccupied, "Sorry, I wasn't sure if you'd come today."

"To tell you the truth, neither was I, but I'm glad I did. This place, it's amazing." She said as she drifted over to a lovely curling, bluish vase made of glass.

"I try to pick pieces that are conductors of energy."

She stopped focusing on the beauty of the items around her, then looking at him curiously, "Conductors of energy?"

"Yes, you could feel it when you walked in."

She answered thoughtfully. "I felt light, and yes, I guess you could call it energy."

"Everything carries its own energy, and some objects serve as conductors. It's beneficial to any environment it's placed in."

She turned to him, smiling. Clearly, he was quite serious. "Sounds like you've made a science out of this."

He nodded, "If you had come earlier, I would have taken you to lunch."

"I wasn't really sure what my plans would be today."

There was another bark from toward the back of the expansive shop. "I think Hazel wants to see you as well. Come on. I'll show you the back."

Windows and light were what struck her about the backrooms of Billy Struve's establishment. It was winter, icy and cold outside, but it felt warm here, not just from artificial means. The first room was a stock room with shelves of items that had yet to be placed on display. The next seemed more of a studio — a table for pottery, an easel, and counters for all varieties of work. She was envious. It was charged with energy. Oddly, she could imagine herself having a desk near one of the large windows and writing, writing in a way she'd never been able to before.

He'd disappeared in the front, hearing the chiming of the doors. She was left here, not quite alone. Hazel lay curled up on a bed just under a light wooden table against the wall. Clearly, it was a spot she'd made her own. There were dual impulses she was feeling. One was to bolt and return to the life she knew, forgetting that people lived like this on their own terms. The other, even more, perplexing than the first, was to sit down on the window seat and pull the soft afghan throw that was draped across it lightly across her shoulders and relax — allow herself to let go of all the tenseness and all the baggage from the past she seemed to carry around with her.

She looked up and saw him standing there in the doorway. Again, he'd surprised her while she was deeply enmeshed in her thoughts. He frowned, "All right?" he asked pointedly.

She wondered about a simple question, but what was the answer? "It must be wonderful to work here," she said, side-stepping the question entirely.

"Well, it is great at times. But the retail thing interrupts." He stepped off the small landing and, in a few direct steps, had made it to the space directly in front of her. "So, I have a microwave. How about a cup of mint tea?"

"Sounds nice."

He nodded, turning away from her but then adding just over his shoulder. "Then, after that, maybe you'll answer my question, Helen."

It was disorienting, having her here, having her here after seeing her last night on his patio. He'd done his best. He'd concentrated on sending energy to her, but then he'd done something else, something he wasn't at all sure that he should. He'd brought her here today, funneled all his concentration on luring her to him. Truthfully, for all intents and purposes, he'd felt as though he'd failed until he found her standing in the middle of his shop in an almost mesmerized state.

He debated within. Was it really fair to influence her like this? After all, he wasn't some sort of vampire beckoning his intended victim to his side. He wanted to help Helen. He wanted, and then he stopped. What exactly did he want from her? If it wasn't even clear in his mind, he shouldn't be playing around with her life.

He brought two cups of steaming tea from the small kitchen galley to the studio where he found Helen sitting on the window seat with Hazel curled up beside her as she stroked her. "Now that's a pretty picture," he commented as he handed her the tea.

"It just kind of happened," she said, taking a sip. "It's good. Do you do a lot of painting?"

He'd grabbed one of the metal chairs lurking around the studio and pulled it beside her. "When I'm inspired. The shop brings in enough money that I don't have to paint, but, of course, I have to stay creative, the ener—" Then he stopped.

"The energy," she finished for him.

"I've been bantering that word around a lot today. So—" he said.

"So," she repeated, stroking Hazel's heavy black fur. She felt calmer now, not thinking as much. He could feel it. This place was soothing her, clearly exactly what she needed.

"You seemed very bothered earlier."

She didn't answer at first, just quietly sipping her tea. And he was struck again at how physically beautiful she was, her hands long and elegant, an aura of delicateness and now rather fragileness. "I don't know. Like I said at dinner, I came here to sort some things out, reassess, I guess."

He nodded, "How's that working out?"

She smiled lightly, meeting his eyes with her large green ones. "Good question. Sometimes, I think reliving the past is maybe just that, reliving the past. Doesn't really change anything, just stirs up—"

"Pain?" he asked.

"Maybe, I mean, it's not a huge secret to me why things happened, how they happened. But it is a secret how I can let go of all that."

"Hmm, there's the trick."

Her long elegant hand started to scratch Hazel just under the ear, and she settled against Helen as though she was in bliss — odd to be jealous of his own dog. "You seem to have made peace with things, William." He felt a bit startled. The last person who called him William was Sara Morgan, his teacher. But here in the small town of Crystal Springs, he was just Billy or Struve to some. Her eyes widened. She was perceptive. "I'm sorry. Would you rather I call you Billy?"

He smiled, shaking his head, "No, no, William is fine. Um, oh yeah, making peace with things — that's a bit of a tall order. I don't know if you can ever completely get rid of the old stuff. I don't know if we're meant to. It kind of reminds us of where we've been, who we've been — a benchmark, so to speak. But it's important to learn from it but not to keep beating yourself up for it. After all, you wouldn't make the same choices today that you did, say, five years ago."

Her eyes were wide and filled with shadows. "I hope not," she murmured.

"And the rest of the cure is living. Just moving on and filling your life with new things, better things that bring you joy."

She sipped her tea, her eyes focusing on something beyond him. She was considering. He could feel it, carefully considering.

She hadn't intended to stay here as long as she had. In fact, she hadn't intended to spend much of any time at all with Billy Struve. But the hours of the afternoon stretched on. There was a comfortable, languid atmosphere throughout the rooms of *Illuminations*. And Helen was not in much of a hurry to relinquish the feeling.

It was approaching four, the hour he would close up shop. There was a door at the back of the store that led to the back patio. While he took care of business up front, Helen wandered outside. It was a bright winter day, and she inhaled deeply. The cool air flooded through her lungs, and she felt peace float in, a peace she had never comprehended as possible.

He appeared in the doorway, quietly waiting for her to notice his presence. "So," he said quietly. "All closed up."

She smiled, "So soon?"

"Well, I'm the owner. It's my prerogative." He walked out further onto the patio. "And today feels like other things take precedence."

"I hope I'm not interfering with your business."

He nodded, "You are, but it's not unwelcome. So, can we try dinner again?"

Her head swirled a bit. It was not unexpected, but it still caught her off guard, "Dinner?"

He smiled, "Yes, but at my place. You know, Hazel and me."

"Um, I don't know."

"Too late to be cautious. We've spent the afternoon together."

"Oh, you think it's too late, do you?"

"I think it's time to let things follow their course. Don't you, Helen?"

Her heart was hammering in her chest a bit more profoundly. But she didn't want to think about it too much. She didn't want to let go of the peacefulness wrapping around her like a cocoon. So, all she said was, "I suppose not."

It struck a chord. They'd stopped on the way to William's house at a small grocery just a few blocks from *Illuminations*. It was like everything else she'd seen of Crystal Springs, homey, personal, and creative. The owner knew Billy Struve on a first name basis. She waited in the café portion of the store with Hazel while he shopped. Mr. Deangelis, the owner, and his daughter came from inside the store to greet her and play with Hazel. It seemed no problem for the dog to be there. It was so different, so alien for her. Where she came from, people were generally aloof, and you'd never see a dog in a grocery. Oddly enough, it felt destabilizing. When William returned to her, he looked at her with concern, "Something wrong?" he asked. "You look a little pale."

"I'm just tired," she lied. And he looked unconvinced. It was second nature for her to cover like this, to cover the truth of her feelings. Why exactly, she'd never particularly examined except that it had begun in her marriage.

"What's wrong?"

"I'm unhappy."

"What's the matter with you? Can't you be satisfied with anything?"

And then it became, *"What's wrong?"*

"Nothing, I'm just tired."

But the truth seemed to bring caustic, painful confrontations. So, she began to avoid them. But this man, this one next to her, was not content to accept platitudes.

It was the house, however, that struck a chord. This shook her a bit because it seemed so oddly familiar. When they pulled up in his driveway, it nearly took her breath away. It was a wooden frame house, sort of warm beige in color, the front with several steps leading up to a porch — nestled comfortably in trees surrounding it, protecting it, she thought a bit abstractly. It was lovely, not the most extraordinary house she'd ever seen, but in some other, indefinable way, it was the most extraordinary house she'd seen.

He patted her hand softly, not questioning her this time. "Come on," he said, but she hesitated. She couldn't help it. She knew if she went inside, things would change. That thought resounded through her mind. But then she stepped out of the jeep, knowing that she would. It was inevitable.

She was wandering around his house, and it made him feel odd, as though some electric sort of energy was weaving its spell around them now. He didn't know he would feel this way, didn't really think about it at all.

"*You really don't get it William. When the two of you finally come together, it will be extraordinary and powerful. Change both your lives in ways you can't imagine. Your spirits are a perfect fit, created together for each other.*"

"*That sounds a bit overwhelming,*" he'd told Sara Morgan.

"*I imagine it will be,*" she'd answered. "*But you have never struck me as a man who would shy from a challenge.*"

And here he was, watching Helen Ellis, absolutely incandescent in the way she was subtly connecting with everything around her. It was profound how drawn he was to her, physically and emotionally. He wanted so fiercely to get past all those barriers she'd erected in the name of self-preservation. And he'd only known her for a few days.

"So, what do you think?" he said, wandering into the den where she was standing near the fireplace.

"You have a wonderful place. Did you do this?" she asked in regard to the landscapes that were placed on either side of the fireplace.

He handed her a glass of white wine. "Yes, some of my early work. I hope I've improved."

She shook her head. "They're wonderful, William. They feel peaceful to me," she murmured. Then she looked at him oddly, "Have you found that here? In Crystal Springs, peace?"

He sat down slowly on the small moss-green sofa. "Sometimes, Helen, I think peace is something you have to work at. It's something earned, not just a natural state of being."

She nodded, sipping her wine. "I guess that's why I don't have it. I never thought I'd have to earn it."

"Well, it helps when you're in a place you want to be, doing things because you enjoy them, not just because you have to."

"Is that what you think I'm doing?"

"Actually, I was talking about myself. I had to remove myself from an environment that was, well, toxic to my spirit. That was the first step for me, I guess, caring for my inner self."

"Some of us don't have that luxury."

"Some of us don't give ourselves the luxury."

She turned away from him, facing his pictures again. He stood up and walked over to her, touching her shoulder. He could feel it, fear. Her experiences had taught her fear. "I'm sorry, Helen. I didn't mean to upset you."

"We're just very different, William. Come from different places," she murmured.

He put his glass of wine on the mantle and put both hands on her shoulders, beginning to gently rub, trying to drive some of her tenseness away. "I'd like to help you relax, Helen," he said. But she didn't answer. He could feel so much, just connecting with her skin — confusion, tumultuous emotion, but it was helping. She was calming. "That's it," he said.

"William," she began.

"Just relax, Helen." She was leaning back against him a bit, not realizing at all what she was doing. It was completely unconscious. He breathed deeply, feeling it as a languid and, yes, sensual feeling traveling through his veins. Sara had said they would be powerful together, but he hadn't realized to what degree. There was a decision to be made now: move forward or wait, giving her a bit more time.

He pulled his hands away from her shoulders and whispered into her ear. "I better get dinner going."

She straightened up, turning around to face him, "Yeah, sorry, that felt good."

He smiled, "Just relax awhile. I'll be in the kitchen."

He headed out the room, trying to shake the almost overwhelming need that was coursing through him.

William had a lovely natural wood dinette in a small sunroom just off the kitchen. But instead, they ate in the den on the coffee table, sitting cross-legged on his large Aztec pattern rug in front of a crackling fireplace. Of all things, he'd made spaghetti, but it was actually quite good.

"This is really good. When did you learn to be a great cook?"

He laughed, "Well, I'm not a great cook, but generally out of necessity. After my marriage fell apart, I decided either I would learn to cook decently or eat takeout for the rest of my life."

"That makes sense." She picked up her glass of wine off the coffee table to take a sip. Her plate was somewhat precariously perched on her lap, but truth be told, she didn't care. This was her second glass of wine. Her limit usually was one, but she felt warm, cozy, and watchful of Hazel, who more than once had tried to abscond with her dinner. "I can't believe Christmas is in two days."

"It's true, any regrets?"

"You mean coming here?"

"Not being with your family."

"No, oddly enough, it feels right. I guess, though, I feel some pressure not doing what I feel I should be doing."

He put his glass down abruptly on the coffee table. "Okay, you'll have to explain that one to me. Not doing what you feel you should be doing?"

She laughed. It was true. Once she voiced it, it sounded remarkably nonsensical. "Okay, let's see. Christmas comes with pressure. You feel if you don't celebrate it in a certain way, you've failed somehow."

"Wow, that sounds joyous!"

"Now you know what I mean. If you don't have a tree," she gestured to the small live pine tree he had in one corner of his house, sparsely decorated with ornaments from his shop. "If you don't have a family around you, if you don't exchange presents, if you don't send out Christmas cards."

"You send out Christmas cards?"

She sighed, "I used to when Kev—" then stopped.

William put his basically cleaned plate onto the coffee table. "Okay, you want to finish that thought?"

She swallowed, good question. Did she really? "I was going to say I did when Kevin and I were together, then for a few years after. I guess to make it seem like I was okay, then I let it go."

"I see, and all this was because you felt you should."

"It's part of the trappings of Christmas. Come on. Didn't you send out Christmas cards when you were married?"

"Honestly, I think Laura did, but I let her handle all that stuff, I'm ashamed to say."

"I see, a bit of a workaholic husband."

He nodded, "Yeah, ambitious, self-centered, all the trappings that go with it. It isn't a wonder she left me." He took a sip of his wine.

"I'm sorry. I didn't mean to make you think about unhappy things."

"No, no, she did me a favor. Made me wake up, re-examine things."

"Did you ever try to reconcile, I mean, once you changed things?"

He shook his head. "No, Helen. One thing I've learned emphatically is that not everyone is a good match for you. Two people can be very nice, but once you put them together, they just don't bring out the best in each other."

"Sounds like you believe in soul mates."

He smiled, "That's one word. Kindred is another. Twins, twin spirits, is another."

"Then I wonder why so many people wind up with the wrong match?" she said softly.

"It's all about learning, Helen. We're all here on this earth to learn and to evolve. And that's hard to do if you always do things perfectly."

She glanced at a clock on the wall. It was already eight. The evening had been flying by, great food, great conversation, and she wasn't in all that much hurry to return to her lonely cottage. They'd just had coffee, and she knew she should leave. "Ah, I see, thinking about leaving now." He spoke from across the den.

"You know, sometimes I get the strange feeling you're reading my mind."

He walked in further, coming to stand just next to her near the fireplace. "Would that I could, my dear," he said laughing.

"I really should get back."

"Because you think that is what you should do, Helen?"

It was awkward. He was too honest, too unvarnished about what he was thinking. "I had a lovely time. In fact—" then she stopped.

"You know, before you vanish back into your old life, it is my quest, my most earnest desire, to get you to say what you really mean."

She frowned, "Are you implying I'm insincere?"

"No, I'm saying you're guarded and defensive and protective of yourself. But you don't have to be around me." He reached out and softly touched her face with the tips of his fingers. It made her literally catch her breath.

"I wanted to say that I can't remember, at least not for a very long time, having such a wonderful evening."

He nodded, "That's high praise, and may I say I feel the same."

He moved a step closer, and her heart began to race. "William, I—" she tried to say, but he was touching both sides of her face now with his hands, softly caressing. "You said you were only offering friendship," she murmured.

"I know, we can be friends, and more," he whispered.

She thought to answer, but then she didn't because he was kissing her now. Softly at first, so gently he eased her into an embrace. And then more intensely, as he folded her deeply in his arms, against his chest, more passionately. It was unexpected and yet more than reasonable.

He drove around the city after he brought Helen home. He was rattled, completely overwhelmed, but delightfully so. *"It's control that you need to work on, William,"* Sara Morgan had said.

"I don't know what you mean. I'm always in control of myself, my life."

"That's the problem," she'd said. *"You have to learn to let go, allow life to flow without you impeding it."*

He hadn't really understood what she'd meant until tonight. He felt as though he were caught in a tidal wave. Helen would have stayed with him at his house. He was sure of it. She was caught up just like he was in the passion igniting between them, the electric crazy flow of energy. She would have stayed, against her better judgment, against what she believed she should do, and all of that would have come crashing down on her the next morning. She wasn't ready for this. Hell, he wasn't ready for this. But it didn't matter, not really, because it was going to happen. The feelings, the sensations, the connection was like a deluge. It wouldn't be denied. But tonight, he'd pulled back. And he didn't know at all if he was happy about it or not. She'd seemed confused, scattered. But once he'd brought her back, he'd stepped into the cottage, closing the door behind him.

Her eyes were wide, with a bit of surprise. But he pulled her, without asking, straight into his arms again, kissing her softly but trying to stave off the intense passion. "I want to see you tomorrow," he'd said.

She was breathing deeply, "I don't know." She was confused, but he wouldn't let her pull away from him now.

"It's all right, Helen," he whispered into her hair. "Don't worry. I'll call you tomorrow." She nodded, and again, he kissed her. This was crazy. All he wanted to do was scoop her up and take her back to his house, into his bed — such an incredibly powerful need.

But he didn't, instead he wandered the darkened streets of Crystal Springs, trying, trying to get a handle on things.

Helen woke from a heavy sleep. It was late for her, ten o'clock, but she felt well-rested and calm. As she wandered around the small cottage, it distantly registered in her mind that it was Christmas Eve. Presents weren't something she needed to worry about. She'd mailed a package filled with them up to North Carolina. But then of course, there was one person she hadn't bought anything for yet — William.

Her breath hitched a bit in her throat at the memory of last night. It was the point at which their understanding of friendship had evolved into what she could only describe as passion, uncontrolled passion. She watched the small coffee pot that the cottage provided slowly drip. Coffee was such a wonderful aroma. It connected her with peaceful, soothing things. There were actually just four more days that she would spend in Crystal Springs. The time was flying now.

She poured herself a cup of the morning brew and curled up in the overstuffed chair. She didn't want to think too much about the future or the past. She wanted to just allow herself to feel, to feel joy.

Her cell phone rang, and she answered without even looking at the number.

"Hello."

"Hello back, and how are you this morning?"

She sipped her coffee, "Good, kind of lazy though. I only got up a little while ago."

William laughed a bit on the other end. "Well, maybe you needed the rest. I was hoping you'd meet me for lunch. We're closing early today because it's Christmas Eve."

She straightened up, thinking about the gift she had yet to buy for him. "Are all the stores closing early?" she asked.

"All of them around here. Why? Have some last-minute shopping to do?"

"Well, some."

"There's still a little of the morning left. Do your shopping, then meet me at the store. Can't wait to see you."

It felt like butterflies, and she was much too old for butterflies. "Okay, that sounds good."

"Great, see you later."

"Okay," she'd already said that, just like a flustered teenager. And then she hung up.

She looked up at the clock, ten-thirty, enough time to hop in the shower and then make a mad dash into town. She wasn't thinking, wasn't examining too much. That, she felt acutely, would ruin everything.

He watched the clock. The morning was busy enough, a steady stream of customers to distract him. But then, it was eleven and eleven-thirty, and his mind wandered, lingering on the wild energy last night passing around them, through them, within them — when he touched Helen, when he kissed her. He'd been warned of it but still hadn't really expected it.

"When the two of you come together, it will be extraordinarily powerful." Sara Morgan had told him serenely as though it was quite natural.

He'd frowned at her somewhat. It was undeniable. At that point in his life, there was still a hefty dose of pessimism within him. "What do you mean powerful?"

She'd smiled at him almost indulgently. "William when two spirits reunite who are a perfect match, it is extraordinary. Energy is created, healing occurs. And there is a need between them to be together that is like an unstoppable storm. It will defy logic, judgment, and reasoning. It is simply undeniable."

And then she'd said something odd that he'd forgotten. "I envy you, William, what is to come. Don't let anything come between you, especially yourselves."

"Especially yourselves," he murmured to himself. Yes, he could easily see that possibility looming — fear, wounds from the past, and a host of other things perceived as stumbling blocks. But if he'd learned anything in his years of life, it was that perception did not necessarily equal truth.

The front bell chimed, and Helen crossed the threshold of *Illuminations*.

She was holding a small decorative bag and smiling as she approached him.

"So," he said, kissing her softly on the cheek, "what's in the bag?"

"None of your business," she laughed. And he knew it was a Christmas gift for him. The truth was he'd already picked one out for her on the first day they'd met on the beach.

There was a change. At first, he'd felt it, then he'd seen it in Helen's aura — the colors of the energy around her. When he'd first met her, in fact, before he'd even introduced himself that first day on the beach, he'd taken a moment to look at her, really look at her. Seeing auras wasn't something that had come easily to him. It began first by picking up random splashes of energy on people and objects. At first, he'd thought it was his vision going, but an eye doctor confirmed this was not the case. Ever since he was a child, he'd had extremely good vision, which hadn't changed as he got older. So, he'd mentioned it to Sara Morgan in one of their sessions, and she had introduced him to the world of energy, the colors of energy, and its significance.

And with much-practiced meditation, he'd begun to see clearly the auras surrounding people.

Helen had been low on energy and surrounded by great splashes of pink and orange. The pink denoted confusion within her emotions, and the orange had a strong connection to other people who might be influencing her. But rather quickly, over the last few days of their association, he noticed a difference: less pink, less orange, more white, and blue-green

— strong energy colors. There was a lighter mood to her, more buoyant. And with no humbleness, he knew he could claim credit, or, rather, their association could. They were helping each other already because he also could feel the energy shifting within him for the better.

He'd just closed the shop, and they were sitting in the back room with Hazel at their feet.

"So, what do you want for lunch?"

She smiled, "This is your town. What do you recommend?"

He grabbed her hand and impulsively brought it to his lips, kissing it softly. "Well, we can pick up some po'boys at a little seafood place, I know, then go picnic somewhere."

"Sounds nice," she murmured. But it was clear her focus was on the hand he was still holding. He breathed deeply. It was difficult. Last night, they'd pretty much let the genie out of the bottle, and now. Well, it seemed as though there was no going back. Again, he brought her hand up to his lips, kissing it more lingeringly this time.

"Or we could go back to my house, and I'll fix us something." She breathed deeply, and it felt like a spell wrapping around them.

"What are we doing?" she whispered softly but with intent.

He shook his head. "I'm not really sure, Helen Ellis. It feels a bit like falling, but not in a bad way." He turned her arm a bit and now softly brought her wrist to his lips.

"You know, this isn't really like me."

"This isn't like anything. This is all brand new." And then he reached over, softly drawing her to him, and began kissing her. He kissed her again and again, and he could feel she was not holding anything back. "Let's go," he whispered to her. He thought he read some confusion in her eyes, but then it was gone, just acceptance. She nodded, and he stood up, soon after pulling her to her feet.

She was going to have an affair. This was the only way Helen could interpret what was happening. It didn't fit into any other construct she had been taught since she was a child.

Of course, it was still new to her. She'd never had an affair, although there had been a few opportunities. Several she could remember after her divorce from Kevin. And she had considered it. She was lonely, feeling terrible about herself, but something had held her back — something that clearly was not holding her back now.

They were largely silent as they drove to William's house. Hazel barked occasionally from the back seat, and once William had reached over to squeeze her hand. "Okay?" he'd said.

She nodded, saying nothing. She was afraid a bit, but it had such an edge of excitement, like the unknown. This was her plunging into the unknown, whatever it might bring, but feeling intoxicatingly alive. They pulled into his driveway, and he turned off the car. But he made no move to get out. Finally, after a few moments, he spoke, "I guess I should ask you if you're sure you want to do this," he murmured.

She waited, smiling a bit. "Was that a question?" she couldn't help but say.

He turned to her, also smiling. "I think that was the lawyer in me trying to cover the bases."

She nodded, "I'm sure."

He seemed to breathe a slight sigh of relief. Then he opened his door and stepped out of the car. She did the same. Her answer had been true. She was sure. Whatever would come, whatever it would bring, she was sure. Breathing in the cool mist around her, she noted happily that around them, it was a sunny day.

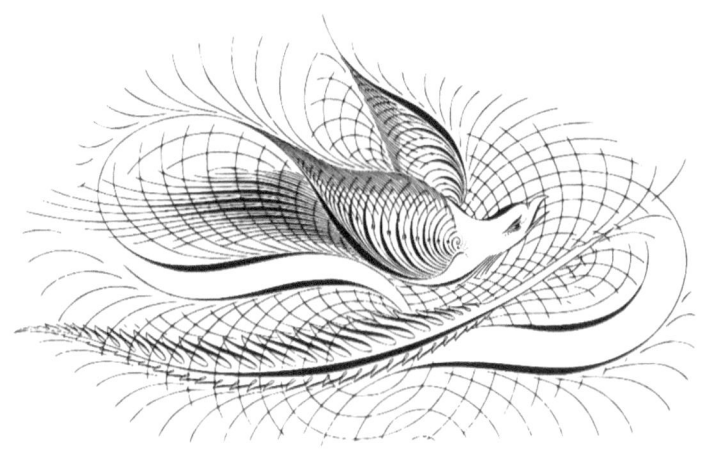

What is Circumspect?
by Sophie Wilde

"What is circumspect?" by Sophie Wilde.

"Hmm," she murmured aloud, ever so lightly tapping her fingertips on the keyboard. Lightly tapping but not really making contact. Not really allowing thoughts to mesh with concrete words.

"Deep sigh," she expounded again aloud. For this had become a habit. There was no one to listen.

October 2:

Here I am, alone on the very second day of the experiment. The first day didn't count. It was too busy stocking up on eatables from the grocery, eatables for a month. One month alone, Sophie Wilde, with no human contact except a fifteen-minute conversation every night with your editor on Skype.

She stopped typing.

"And again, whose brilliant idea was this?"

"Oh yes, that's right, mine." Restlessly, she strummed her fingers across the keyboard as if it were some kind of piano. The house around her creaked. It was windy. It was October in a hundred-year-old farmhouse on the coast of Virginia, and its walls creaked. Its doors creaked; not much in the house didn't creak.

Evening 8:30 PM on the dot:

"How's your first night, Sophie?"

His name was Stephen Archer, and he smiled broadly. He was a youngish, divorced guy about fortyish, five to seven years older than she and not bad-looking, although, until just this moment, she hadn't taken the time to notice.

"You are paying me for this? And it's the second night."

"You bet, baby. Any insightful observations or just vacant ramblings on your first night alone?"

That's right. He always called her baby. That's why she hadn't noticed if he was good-looking.

"Second night, Stephen."

He nodded and grinned, and took a sip from a beer bottle. Damn, she hadn't bought beer, but wine, yes, wine, and a bottle of bourbon.

"So you're all stocked up, sweetheart."

She sighed, "Yeah." She'd thought he might not be so irritating across so many hundreds of miles. "Yeah, all snug as a bug, Stephen."

Midnight or so,

She kept a journal beside her bed, the old-fashioned kind with pen and paper. She'd moved into the house, completely furnished; this old farmhouse that Stephen Archer had rented for her from just a photo off the internet. She clearly remembered that curious conversation from some months ago in his Richmond office.

"So, do you think solitude makes people crazy?"

She looked at him quizzically. Although over time, she'd come to feel she really didn't look at him at all. "Depends on the person, depends on the solitude," she delivered rather slowly and decisively. In dealing with men, particularly in the workplace, she'd found it imperative to be exact and never hesitate. Otherwise, they would intuit it as some sort of softness.

He stared at her keenly for a moment as though considering, but she tried not to notice too much. She'd made a practice of never looking at him too closely. "So, Sophie Wilde, I've come up with an idea if you're not too faint of heart to give it a try."

She frowned. Faint of heart? Clearly, he was trying to push her buttons.

"What idea?" she said curtly, but with enough off-handedness to make it clear she didn't expect too much.

He smiled again, and she did happen to catch his expression this time. He seemed amused, like the cat with the mouse exactly where it wanted it. "Halloween's coming up. How about I stick you in some old isolated farmhouse near the Rappahannock for the month? You keep to yourself completely and send me an interesting column at the end of each week."

"You're kidding," she said blandly.

He nodded, "Hey, if you're concerned, I could send Sam or one of the other boys."

She sighed deeply. "But what if there's just nothing interesting to report."

He nodded, "Well then, it's a little getaway for you on my dime. And no TV or radio."

And no shopping or visits to any stores. That's why the big stock up, just nothing but her and the house. Of course, walks were allowed, but no visiting. She'd just be the eccentric recluse who moved into the neighborhood for a month.

She stared at the blank page. She should write something, record something, but she'd never been particularly enthusiastic about diaries.

I don't like my room.

She scribbled down with irritation.

The Master bedroom on the second floor is filled with antique cherry wood furniture, and the other two bedrooms are completely empty. So much for being furnished, and she used that word loosely. So she'd designated one empty room as her yoga room, and the other had yet to be labeled. But she'd brought her sheets and satin comforter from home, her apartment in Richmond. They lent comfort. They connected her to what she really was.

Third Day:

She walked through the graveyard at dusk. There was actually a graveyard not far from her house behind an old Baptist church. For the most part, she expected that it would be quiet and unoccupied. "Does solitude drive people crazy?" It was a question that she turned over in her mind as she watched the light slowly eke out of the cloudy sky overhead. She'd wrapped herself in a crocheted black shawl inherited from her grandmother upon her death. Her sisters had wanted jewelry and china, and she had wanted the shawl. It felt like her grandmother, carried her stillness.

She walked, the earth beneath her feet crunching with the leaves that had already begun to fall. *How did you get here, Sophie Wilde?* She whispered to herself.

A breeze cascaded through her blonde hair that she'd pulled into a loose bun. And then she stopped. Just a few yards away, a man was kneeling near one of the tombs. He seemed consumed with his own thoughts and hadn't even looked up to note her approach. So, as quietly as she could, she turned and headed in the other direction.

"Please don't leave."

She froze in her steps. Remember, remember reclusive, she turned slowly again. He was standing up now beside the tomb — an odd-looking fellow with long brown hair just past his shoulders. He was dressed in strange attire, some sort of suit but clearly antiquated. "I didn't want to disturb you," she called out.

He began to walk toward her, and she felt a nervousness flutter up to her heart. Was this visiting — a random conversation at dusk in a cemetery? He had a beard and mustache that were not clean-cut like Stephen Archer's, although somehow neat in its flamboyance. "Disturb me?" he smiled, pausing just a few feet away from her. "There isn't much here except you and your thoughts. It's refreshing to see another face."

She pulled her grandmother's shawl more tightly about her, feeling a chill pass through her in the night air. "I was just taking a walk."

"You live in the old Greenwall house."

"Um, you mean the farmhouse."

"Yes, just down the road."

"I didn't know it had a name. I'm only there for a month. In fact, I should get back."

He nodded, glancing around them, "Perhaps you should. It's getting late, Miss."

He waited. He was waiting for her name. And she wondered if she should give it. Things tended to change once you gave a name. "Sophie Wilde."

"Yes, Sophie Wilde, just so you know. It isn't wise to be about at night here. The land is still untamed. I'll walk you home."

She felt trapped. She was breaking the rules, but how could she refuse? How indeed?

Evening, 8:30 PM:

"How you holding up, princess?"

Stephen Archer was munching on a bag of potato chips. He was probably working late to meet a deadline, and that possibility reminded her of how she ached to be back in the city. "Nothing much to report."

He glanced up from something on his desk he was examining while waiting for an answer. "Really? Nothing? Hmm, this could all be a bust."

"Yes, it could be an entire waste of time." It hadn't even crossed her mind to tell him about the man she'd met in the cemetery, the man who'd walked her home at a brisk pace, the man whose name she hadn't even asked for and who hadn't offered it. While, of course, he had hers.

"Well, I expect some creativity this weekend for your column."

"I'm sure I'll come up with something."

He grinned, although she felt keenly his mind was elsewhere. "I'm counting on it."

Seventh Day:

Life has settled into a maudlin routine. And tonight, her column was due. So, she'd decided on the topic of memory — memory and how it fills the spaces when so many aspects of life become empty.

She had avoided going out after her last encounter except for quick walks thoroughly up and down the road where the farmhouse lay. It was odd, for much of the day, a quiet road, and then once in a while, vehicles, mostly trucks bent on arriving at some other destination, came zooming down it at such a pace that someone could easily be killed if they took a false step. Clearly, this wasn't a destination, just a space that people hurriedly passed through.

Memory — back to topic.

The largely empty farmhouse held several rooms upstairs. The one designated for yoga held the engagement.

That particular bundle of memories had taken up approximately three years of her life around the age of twenty-five: two years of courtship, one of engagement, and its aftermath.

Of course, it wasn't something that would be spoken about in her column, just the idea that memories in solitude take on a larger shape and begin to breathe and walk like living things. Was this madness? Was this the beginning of madness or just the natural order of life? Where there is space, it will be filled with something. The absence of living makes room for the past to live again.

That was good. She'd use that.

8:30 evening:

She mailed her column earlier in the afternoon and rewarded herself afterward with a walk in the cemetery. It was close to dusk, but this time, it was empty. She passed the grave where he'd been standing. *Amelia Lecord, died 1937*. Odd, perhaps an ancestor.

"Hmm, some strange introspection, Sophie Wilde. Are you sure you're doing all right there?"

She wrapped her grandmother's shawl more tightly around her. There was a chill in the house tonight. "You didn't like it?"

"No, it was genius. You should write a book. Why don't you spend your time writing a book?"

She shrugged. How odd to be so disconnected from her only human contact, well, lately, anyway.

"I don't know."

"You know you should. You run very deep. There's a market for that out there."

She smiled, but it was all fatigue.

She entered the engagement room just to look and see what was still there. As she walked within her mind, like a broad expanding canvas, she could see the lovely Victorian house they'd picked out for the reception. It would be decorated with violets and pale pink roses. "Will your fiancé be joining you today?"

She walked through the room, imagining what it would have looked like and how it would have smelled—fragrances.

It was cruel of her to come here, to come here, to put herself through this. But she wanted to just touch the texture of her dream before it was taken.

"No, he won't be."

And then she'd turned and left without a word. And called later and canceled everything.

The following evening at 8:30 PM:

"I never asked you, Sophie. How come you're not married or claimed?"

"That's personal."

"I suppose, but given our odd arrangement, I thought we could share a bit."

She looked at him — his face, his expression, placid, calm, and unreadable. "I was engaged. It fell apart."

He nodded, "He cheated on you?"

Her eyes widened. How could he — "Why would you say that?"

"You know it's funny I have a barometer for people. And you, you're very mistrustful. Something must have made you that way."

"Maybe."

"Yeah, maybe."

Tenth Day:

She'd thrown a blanket across the wooden floor of the second room. There was something fascinating about an empty room, even devoid of draperies — just silent, open, echoing. She sat cross-legged at the center. She'd already spoken to Stephen that evening. It was clear he was anxious to go. He had dialed in from home, probably on his way out to meet someone, maybe a date, maybe a group of friends. There were a few friends she had left behind, some family. Told them all she was going into seclusion for a month, and they'd accepted it more readily than she'd expected.

"Perhaps you should take some time to re-evaluate your life, Sophie, to see what you really want. I think you've been in a rut for a while."

That was her mother. Her mother had applauded the break-up of her engagement, but somewhere along the way had decided the road to liberty was being in a rut.

She closed her eyes and breathed deeply, clearing away the rubbish, only allowing her mind to soak up what was around her. And then, in the distance, she heard a strange tapping from downstairs. She opened her eyes, staring at the doorway. Maybe it was a branch rubbing the house somewhere. It was a windy night. So she waited, and it continued.

She stood up and headed down the steep stairs of the Greenwall house. The staircase in itself was horrible, horribly steep. At the top, you could see your way straight down. A fall or a misstep would be damaging. She made her way carefully, tentatively, expecting all would be resolved by the time she was finished. But as her bare feet touched the first floor of the house, she recognized what it was. Knocking — someone was knocking at the front double doors.

They led onto a screen porch at the front of the house. One that she wasn't at all sure she had locked up tonight. She might not have. She couldn't remember.

Again, the knocking jolted her. She was alone here, alone in the house, this quiet, deserted place.

And then a pause at the door — she breathed deeply, waiting silently. She wouldn't answer, and they would go away.

She stood frozen behind the double doors, waiting, waiting.

Then quietly but strongly, "Sophie, Sophie Wilde, I've come to check on you. A storm is coming."

It was him. She recognized the voice, the man from the cemetery. "I'm all right." She spoke through the door. "You don't need to worry."

There was quiet. Maybe he'd left, moved on. But then again, "It's all right, Sophie. It's all right to let me in, you know. I won't hurt you."

Her hand brushed the door. Two minds, the city girl would be insane to let anyone in now, and the other — the one caving to the solitude, caving inwardly, collapsing. "I can't now. Thanks for the warning."

"Take out your candles and your flashlights. You may lose your lights."

Her heart was hammering with fright, with confusion. "Thanks, I will.

And then she heard the quick slam of the screen door on the porch as he left. She should go out and lock it, but she wouldn't. She pulled a chair in front of the doors in the slender hallway. She would sleep in the living room on the sofa with candles and flashlights tonight.

Eleventh Day:

She walked around the house at mid-morning to inspect if there was any damage. Power had gone off from around midnight until five or so in the morning. As she walked around the house she picked up stray branches that had been downed here and there. She wore short boots that crunched in the masses of fallen leaves. It didn't seem too terrible. There was some stray debris on the roof but not enough to cause serious concern.

As she turned the corner of the property, she saw him approaching across the field. The man from the cemetery dressed just the same as the first time she'd met him. She could retreat into the house. It would be rude, but it would maintain her contractual isolation. But she didn't. She stood there, the branch still in hand, and waited.

"Sophie Wilde, I'm glad to see you braved the storm well," he said as he crossed the final distance between them.

"Yes, it wasn't too bad, although I lost power."

He stopped in front of her maybe a yard's distance between them. He was actually in the very same clothes, that short leather burgundy-colored jacket, but antiquated in style, dark pants, and a white shirt. "I do want to apologize. I think I frightened you at your door last night."

She smiled, "Yes a bit. I'm a city girl. You can't be too cautious."

He nodded, "Yes, and you are in the house alone, in a vulnerable position." She glanced away feeling uncomfortable at his odd comment. "It was kindly meant, though."

She turned back to him, suddenly struck by a thought. "You know I don't even know your name."

"No, I suppose we haven't been properly introduced. But perhaps if you're kind enough to offer me a cup of coffee, we can remedy that."

There was a heavy wooden table in the dining room, a very rustic piece in the style of a long picnic table made out of dark wood. Sophie had served the coffee there and perched on one side on its long bench while Mr. Joshua Thorn was on the other. Odd in the daylight hours she felt no trepidation about inviting him in. But last night, well then, it had been inconceivable. "I see, so you write for this newspaper in the city," he inquired.

"Yes, for about five years now. While I'm here, I send in a column at the end of each week. It was my editor's idea."

"And I'm here now helping you break the rules."

She smiled at his disarming frankness, a bit astonished at how refreshing it was to talk to someone face-to-face. "Well, the rules were a bit opaque, and I consider them open to interpretation."

He was an unusual man, Joshua Thorn. He had pulled his long hair back today in a ponytail — a style that oddly seemed to suit him. He wore a beard and mustache, but they were well-kept, keeping with that out-of-synch aura that he seemed to project. "I'm sorry. Where do you live exactly?" she asked.

"Not very far. I have a place on the other side of the cemetery."

"Well, I appreciate the warning last night. I hope you weren't' insulted by my reaction."

He smiled again as though he somehow found her amusing, "It was natural, Sophie Wilde. Now let me ask you. Are you planning to tell your editor friend about me?"

She sipped her coffee, not really having considered that possibility at all. "I don't know."

Eleventh Day — later:

Journal Entry: Secrets — The Nature of and Purpose of

She was only halfway into the month and had already broken the cardinal rule. No relationships with the outside world. She was ostensibly not in too deep to turn around and establish boundaries.

"Why don't you grace me with your presence tonight? I'll fix you an early dinner at my house?"

It was so odd, and it was difficult to tell him no. He was charming, so charming in that old world way of his, so mannered, so compelling. She'd paused in her writing. How long had it been since she'd actually been attracted to a man — not since her debacle of an engagement? She'd closed herself off, just as she was in this house, sealed off from life.

But he was here too in her isolation, a breath of hope. Why shouldn't she?

"I can't," she'd answered.

And then he smiled as though it was not unexpected. "I see Sophie Wilde, the rules. You're breaking them but not too much."

She nodded, "Yes, not too much."

She dropped the pen. She hated writing by hand.

And then he'd said something else, something odd. "So I wonder if there is another storm tonight, and I come by knocking again if you'll abide my entrance or not."

It was an odd, awkward moment. She was not at all sure what he meant, if it was innocent or if it was not innocent at all. So she hadn't answered. And then he'd left. He must have gone, although oddly, now she didn't remember him leaving. She wasn't sleeping well, not well at all. It must be that.

8:30 PM:

"I'm beginning to believe this was a mistake."

She stared at the screen a bit blankly. Her thoughts were elsewhere. She thought about the unnamed room upstairs – the other was *The Engagement,* but that one, maybe that one, was *Secrets.*

"Sophie," his voice was louder, more emphatic. She surfaced from her thoughts.

"Yes, sorry, Stephen."

"I said this might be a mistake."

She stared at him a bit more blankly, feeling a pull elsewhere again. "Why would you say that?"

"You are being careful? Locking doors and such?"

A slight chill crossed the threshold, crossed and prickled her skin. "Yes, of course, why are you asking?"

"I don't want to worry you, but I believe it's best to be aware. There have been some deaths a few miles away from you, closer to the town."

She straightened up, fear suddenly bringing her back in connection to the present. "You mean murders?"

He frowned. Was that such a difficult question? "Hard to say yet. There has been no cause of death found, just two people. One in a field and one in their house, dead — inexplicably. Do you want to call this off?"

She thought about her room upstairs, just named *Secrets,* as of yet unexplored — tantalizing. Did she want to call this off? "Not yet, Stephen, not just yet."

Oct. 13:

Journal Entry

Yesterday, it rained, and I spent much of the day sleeping. Strangely, for no reason, I seemed abnormally tired. I tried to consider what Stephen had said about the deaths in the area, but for some reason, I felt disconnected from it. It doesn't feel at all real to me. This solitude has touched me in a curious way, as though I'm a fraction of a step somewhere else from everyone and everything else.

"Do you believe in other dimensions?"

Joshua Thorn smiled oddly at her. It was nearing dusk, and on impulse, she'd decided to take a walk in the cemetery. The weather had dipped a bit, and the wind was blowing more brutally. And she wasn't at all surprised to find him there, almost as though he expected her. "Other dimensions, Sophie Wilde. Now, that's an odd question. I believe some of us live out of step with everyone else if that's what you mean."

"Some of us?" She asked with curiosity.

"Yes," he nodded, "I include myself in that assessment. Now, whether you join me in that grouping is something you might need to decide."

8:30 PM:

"What do you think of me?"

Stephen Archer looked a bit surprised. It wasn't her nature to engage him in any manner that was remotely personal. "In what respect?"

"In any respect that comes to mind."

He frowned. He was suspicious, cautious, expecting traps where there may be none. "I think you are an amazing writer. You should write a book."

"Really? That's what you think about when you look at me."

He leaned back in his leather swivel chair. He was at the office, late again. And oddly enough she wondered why this evening. "Oh, when I look at you? When I look at you, Sophie Wilde, I think you're beautiful with your blond hair, gray eyes, and lovely body. And I always wonder why you are alone. Then, when you speak, I understand why."

"What does that mean?"

He laughed, "That's it. The aura you give off. The *I'll rip to pieces aura if you get too close.*"

She stood there staring at the screen with her mouth open. She shouldn't have drunk a second glass of wine at dinner. She shouldn't have let Joshua Thorn kiss her goodnight after he walked her home. That was why she panicked. That was why she wanted to connect to her world again through Stephen and ill-advisedly stumbled through this door. "I don't do that," she whispered.

He wasn't smiling now, just staring at her oddly. "Are you ready to come back yet, Sophie?"

"I don't know," she murmured.

Oct. 14: Column Day:

She was spending the morning doing yoga in the room of *Secrets*. She still had no earthly clue why she called it that or if she should continue doing so. The other room – the *Engagement room* – she simply had begun to avoid as though it was tainted somehow. Strange, how an imaginary abstract label could become so tangible to the mind.

She cleared her thoughts, breathing deeply and closing her eyes. She sat on a mat she'd unrolled in the middle of the room with her legs crossed. *"Are you ready to come back yet, Sophie?"* The question still hung out in the air, floating about. Was she? And if she wasn't, why not? Was this solitude beginning to get comfortable for her? All this reflection, inner ramblings — in some respect did she prefer being cut off from the mainstream of life?

She breathed in deeply and then exhaled.

"All worthy questions, Sophie Wilde."

Slowly, she opened her eyes to see Joshua Thorn standing in the doorway of her room.

She felt stunned and confused. "How did you get in?"

"The front door," he murmured. "You left it open."

Her mind went blank. That didn't seem likely. He walked through the doorway and began to circle the room. "I was wondering why you call this the room of *Secrets*. It's fairly empty just now."

"I-I'm not sure."

He continued to look around as he slowly circled her along the walls, gazing out the long window covered by white gauzy shears. "It seems an odd designation. Secrets take up space and time and energy. Perhaps you were thinking of keeping secrets here."

"I don't know. But you are—"

And then he stopped circling and turned to her, "I am one of your secrets? That's right. I am the broken rule."

She took in a breath. "Why are you here?"

He smiled for the first time since he entered the room. "To tell you there's a full moon out tonight. And everything tends to change with the full moon."

She opened her eyes again and the room was empty. The first thing she did was go downstairs to check the front door. She turned its knob, and it opened easily onto the screen porch. It was windy outside and the door there flapped violently ajar in the breeze.

Imagination: The Role of Imagination as It Usurps Memory

She was convinced of it or rather convinced herself of it. The idea that memory, which once had dominance, was now supplanted by imagination—that thing that expands and fills the vacant spaces.

She wrote all morning, expanding her theory until she beat it succinctly into the proper volume of a column. She actually thought it was quite good. Sometime around 1:00 in the afternoon, after she'd emailed it to Stephen Archer, she had time to sit down and really consider what had happened.

How Joshua Thorn had entered her house through a door she'd known to be locked, soundlessly ascended to the second floor of her old horrible creaky house and almost vanished from her sight. Although, in all fairness to what was plausible, he hadn't vanished in front of her just when she'd turned away or closed her eyes. She couldn't absolutely remember.

So had he, had he been here at all or, as her column suggested, been an amplified product of her foolishly indulged imagination? And tracking on that thread, had she met him at all, or was he a figment simply dreamed up to keep her company in her solitude?

She sipped the cup of tea, blueberry tea she'd brewed just fifteen minutes earlier.

If she were to dream up a man to keep her company, what would his attributes be?

Charming? — Yes

Comforting? — Perhaps

Handsome? — Yes, but not in a safe way, in an unusual way

Dangerous? — In some respects, but certainly not to her personally

Mysterious? — She paused. Perhaps she was onto something here. Mysterious? Absolutely. Someone to stimulate her mind. Who had said that — a woman had to first be seduced in her mind and then her body. It was blank. Perhaps it had been her. Did Joshua Thorn fit the bill? Yes he did, which was horribly upsetting. Because if she had simply made him up, then as Stephen Archer had indicated, solitude does indeed induce madness.

So she would do the only thing she could. Wait for tonight, wait and see if there is a full moon, then she will know that the information he gave her was accurate. And he was real.

8:30 PM:

"Well, I give it to you, Sophie, that was a thought-provoking article," and then he hesitated.

She had decided to wait until after their conversation to go out, to go out and look for Joshua's full moon.   .

"Well I'm glad you liked it."

"Liked it? I was riveted. But I have to tell you I've decided to pull the plug on this experiment."

She felt stunned, as though he'd reached through the screen and physically slapped her across the face. "You what?"

His expression was very solemn, grim if you like. It was an expression she rarely remembered seeing on the face of Stephen Archer. "I want you to pack up and be out of there in the morning."

"Why? I thought you liked the columns."

"I do, they're brilliant. But my gut tells me something is very wrong with you."

She couldn't think, and all she could think was the work she'd done. The rooms upstairs, *The Engagement* and *Secrets* which still had to be unraveled. The weaving she done here with her mind, the reality she'd created. It was a web, a massive web she couldn't just walk away from. She shook her head, "No, no, I'm not ready."

"Sophie," he leaned into the screen. His voice was different now—not hard, not biting, but soft and concerned. It's time to come back, Sophie."

She shook her head then closed the computer. She rose from her laptop as though she was in shellshock. And then she picked up the sweater she had laid across the table and put it on. She wouldn't deal with this now. She would go outside to see if it was a full moon.

"It isn't wise to be about at night here. The land is still untamed."

Joshua's words when they first met. But she would just slip out for a few moments, not long. Just to see. It might well be her last chance to see. She walked through the front double doors of the house out onto the screen porch. The sky was pitch black almost except for the dim light of a few stray stars. She could tell from outside, not from the porch, whether the moon was full. So, with shaky fingers, she unhooked the latch to the door and stepped out into the night. The air smelt strange of burning leaves. She moved around the side of the house and in the distance could see a soft glow. Overhead it was cloudy so she walked further toward the light, toward the direction of the cemetery. The burning smell got stronger, and the leaves crunched beneath her boots. She continued to look upward. If she saw it, the moon, she would return home. In the distance, the light continued to glow but fluctuated. The truth seeped in. It was a bonfire. She stopped walking and in the night sky, covered beneath the shifting, mutating clouds she finally saw the moon—the full moon.

"You see, I told you."

She heard the movement behind her, though moments earlier it hadn't been. "What else did I say?" his voice almost rasping in her ears.

"Everything tends to change with the full moon."

She wasn't sure, wasn't at all sure she wasn't speaking to herself. And then she felt the pressure of his hands on her shoulders and his warm breath on her neck. "Yes, yes it does. And now I'll show you why it's the room of Secrets."

And the flames that, moments before, were miles away seemed to be just in front of her eyes.

"Do you think I can take her home soon?"

The doctor looked up from his desk into Mr. Archer's eyes. He certainly didn't want to give him false hope, but there was reason to be optimistic. The new drug had roused his wife out of her catatonic state. He stood up trying to rationalize a way to walk the tightrope between hope and reality. "Mr. Archer, Sophie has made great strides, but she also has created a sort of alternate reality—a bridge, if you will, between where she's been existing and your world. It may take some time before she entirely comes back to us."

"So what do I do in the meantime Dr. Thorn?"

He shrugged, "Honestly, play along. Be comforting and play along. By the way, she's decided I'm some sort of supernatural werewolf creature."

Stephen Archer frowned, "And me?"

"Still her boss, some sort of newspaper editor. But she knows you told her it's time to go home."

"Well that's something."

"Yes in a way it's encouraging. Your wishes have made some impact on her reality."

"You know she was a brilliant writer before the accident."

"Clearly, it's her imagination that has kept her from, well, falling apart. As I said play along."

Stephen Archer nodded, then left the office, heading down the hall to his wife's room.

The rest of the night was a blur. Somehow she had returned to her house. Well, the Greenwall house. She couldn't be at all sure now where home was. Joshua Thorn had brought her into the night, near the wild erupting bonfire. And she'd seen the others dancing with abandon beneath the full moon, writhing and mutating within the flickering shadows. And Joshua Thorn had beckoned her, enticed her to join them. But she'd pulled away running through the darkness in terror, and hearing him, chasing her, him, and then the hot fetid breath of an animal.

Somehow, she'd gotten back into the old house sobbing, blocking the doors. She'd spent the night in terror on the sofa downstairs, not truly getting any sleep until the dawn came creeping through the thin drapes.

She heard a tapping at the door. It was early. She checked her watch, just after seven. She hesitated. It could be Joshua who would drag her back into the darkness. So she just waited, silently hoping whoever it was would just leave, just go away.

"Sophie," she heard a voice through the door.

She shivered. Someone was calling her, but it wasn't Joshua. She rose from the sofa and moved slowly toward the front hallway. Again, a pounding on the screen door. What if it was a trick? What if it was Joshua? He might kill her this time. He might be responsible for the deaths of all those other people. The ones who were just found dead, for no reason, just stopped living. Why would someone do that, just stop living for no reason, as though they'd simply had enough of this world, as though it were just too difficult or too painful to go on?

And then she heard a crash, and she lurched back in fear. Whoever it was had kicked the screen door in. She turned and leaped toward the stairs frantically as she heard another crash as the intruder barreled through the double doors she'd blocked with a chair. She bolted into the room of *Secrets*, to its center. She sat on the floor with her knees drawn up and ducked her head so she couldn't see. If she didn't look, they wouldn't be real — imagination, just imagination.

She heard the creak of the door but kept her head bent down. Perhaps she had created it all, perhaps the moon hadn't been full, or perhaps she had made it so.

"Sophie," a voice said softly. "I told you it was time to leave."

She was crying, crying with fear. All her things, all the things she had created here to keep her safe and warm where would they go when she was gone?

"Sophie," Stephen's voice beside her now. He was kneeling beside her.

"But there are two more columns to finish."

He lightly touched her hair. "I know. If you're not ready, I'll stay here with you until you're done."

She looked into his face, the tears still pouring down her cheeks. "You would do that for me."

He smiled, taking her hand in his. "I would do anything for you."

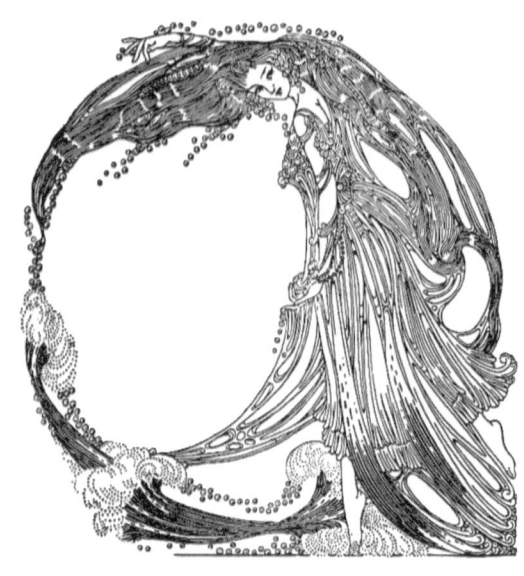

A Few Moments with a Stranger

There was only so much time one could spend doing one's hair and make-up and waiting patiently, impatiently — calmly, with disdain, with distraction. Annabelle Stuart stared in the mirror. She glanced down at her watch — a full 90 minutes until her husband returned from his business meeting to collect her for dinner. Annabelle had just made forty and wondered if she could be going through a mid-life crisis. Was that even possible for women?

She took one last look at herself in the mirror, put on her high heels, and headed downstairs for a pre-dinner drink in a nightclub in the heart of the Royal Orleans.

As she meandered through the lobby in her short black cocktail dress and high heels, she mused again how out of sync this grand old hotel seemed to be with its patrons. The place was historic, grandiose, and plush, yet a modern crowd moved through it largely unaware, as though so self-absorbed, they remained untouched by their surroundings.

It confounded her. How could it be so? For her, the history of the place seeped out of the bricks, mortar, and chandeliers; the fixtures, good and bad, felt nearly suffocating to her. She was overwhelmed and exhilarated on a sensory level but, at the same time, felt nearly crushed by the weight of its impact.

As she settled into a booth at the *Red Room* she sipped her ice-cold Margarita and wondered if perhaps it was simply her own restlessness she was projecting onto the surroundings. There were corners, shadows in her life she didn't wish to examine too closely — in fact, for the most part, didn't want to examine at all.

The dimly lit club inside the Royal Orleans was virtually empty except for a few stray patrons. Again, she checked her watch — an hour and twenty minutes. She sighed so deeply it felt as though it rattled her deepest soul, finally allowing reality to cascade across her. Emptiness it spoke, pervasive, unyielding emptiness.

"I wonder if I might be so bold." It surprised her. She was so entrapped in her thoughts she hadn't noticed anyone approaching the table. She glanced up into the face of a tall, nearly gaunt man — his skin somewhat pale but eyes brown or black, almost mesmerizing in their intensity.

Sheer confusion washed over her. "I'm sorry?" she responded.

The eyes warmed ever so slightly in response. "I was wondering if I might share your company for a time."

Annabelle felt her skin prickle a bit. Was he trying to pick her up? The ring on her finger was plain enough, a smile as though he was reading her thoughts. "I assure you the request is an innocent and honorable one. I saw you sitting here alone and thought how lovely it would be to share some pleasant company."

Listening to him speak so fluidly, it was the first time that it dawned on her that he had an accent, a British accent, to be exact. Again, she considered. He was well-dressed, wearing a dark suit, and looked respectable—well kept—beard and mustache, clean cut, except for his hair. He had quite long hair, longer than her short crop—hair pulled back loosely in a long ponytail.

The moment felt frozen as coherent thought attempted to penetrate her surreal circumstance. Her husband wouldn't like it, wouldn't like it, or wouldn't care. Was there really anything wrong with sharing a few moments with a stranger? She glanced up and smiled.

"I suppose."

He smiled and, in an old-world sort of charming manner, seated himself across from her in the dimly lit lounge. Again, she wondered distractedly if this constituted some sort of betrayal in her marriage, even if she was just sharing the company of another man for a few scattered minutes. There was a time before, many years before, when she would have thought so, as would her husband. "Troubling thoughts?" the stranger asked. There was the light accent, maybe British, maybe more Eastern European, hard to say. She shook her head and sipped out of the defrosting Margarita glass. "No, not really," and then she laughed a bit nervously. "You know I don't even know your name."

She hadn't noticed he had a brandy glass in his hand, a brandy drinker. With her husband, it was Bourbon. She didn't think they'd ever had brandy in the house. "I'm sorry my manners are a bit remiss tonight. My name is Gerard, Gerard St. Clair."

She smiled, "I'm Anabelle Stuart."

He laughed, "Like the poem?"

His voice was low but smooth, smooth like glass, unflawed, swirling glass. "Poem?" she asked a little blankly.

"Yes, it was many and many a year ago in a kingdom by the sea."

"Oh Edgar Allan Poe."

"So you've heard the reference before?"

She shook her head. "Not from anyone else. I mean, I know the poem, but no one has ever connected it with me."

He sipped from the large brandy glass fluidly, easily, as though he were accustomed to doing so. "Well now they have. It suits you, I think, mysterious, and if I'm not too bold, a little tragic."

She laughed unexpectedly, "How charming, you think I'm tragic."

"He shook his head, "No, I think you seem sad, and for a woman as beautiful as you are, that is tragic."

As she sipped her drink, her head was swirling. This wasn't good. She was slipping, slipping into a place where there was comfort in a stranger's words, balm for the pain of disillusionment inside her. It was dangerous. Without even much effort, he was reaching out to her vulnerabilities. "I think we're all sad at one time or another. That's not unusual."

"Depends on the duration," he said with charm.

She swallowed. *Don't open a door and expect to be able to close it again.* Where had she heard that? She'd slipped, let him inside. She should get up and leave now; go back to her room. "Well, I'm just on my own tonight. My husband is in a conference, meetings, and I just wanted to get out of the hotel room. We'll probably have a late dinner." That was good. She was setting up fences now, mentioning her husband.

His dark eyes had never left her face as she spoke. "Well, Annabel Lee, it's unfortunate to be alone on such a lovely night. And where your husband has been remiss has been my blessing, if only to enjoy your company for a limited time." Her heart was thumping now, and she felt dizzy.

"Are you here on business?"

His dark eyes enveloped her. "Pleasure, traveling for pleasure."

She nodded, "How are you enjoying the city?"

"The city? Well, I find it comfortable. It reminds me of Europe, which is so filled with textures and layers of history. It suits me."

His voice was lulling, relaxing, smoothing the edges in her. "You make it sound —" and then she hesitated. "Well, I never looked at it in quite that way."

She sipped her drink. She should go because, and then she remembered. He'd texted her before and probably wouldn't make dinner. She'd have to get something, and he'd see her later. "Annabelle."

She smiled, "Yes."

Slowly, he put the drink in his hand down on the table. "I'd like you to take a walk with me."

Her heart picked up its beat. She was heading in a dangerous direction. If she went, if she went and he asked, she would sleep with him. She'd never had an affair before, but she knew her husband had. She'd forgiven him for it after counseling. She'd forgiven him, but it still chaffed. And she always wondered what he was doing, who he was with. Its specter shadowed them or rather shadowed her. "I'm sorry, Gerard. I don't think I can."

He nodded, "I see, because of your husband?"

"Yes, I suppose."

"And she clings to her sepulchre in her kingdom by the sea."

"What did you say?"

He smiled slowly, "Sorry, the poem. I was just thinking of how we cling to our tragedy because it is familiar."

"So you're saying that I'm clinging to my tragedy."

"To your sadness, your unhappiness, because it's what you know as opposed to the unknown."

"All I did was refuse to take a walk with a stranger."

"All I offered was a walk, Annabelle." He picked up the brandy glass and sipped it again.

It made her feel foolish but also worried. Was he right, just offering an innocent walk? Or was she? He was traveling alone, wouldn't be in the city long, just looking for a brief, inconsequential involvement — if it could be called that.

"You're questioning my motives," he stated plainly.

She smiled a bit tremulously. "I've been married for a while, Gerard. I'm not altogether sure how the world works anymore."

"I've never paid much attention to how the world works, Annabelle."

"Most of us don't have that luxury."

He shrugged, taking a long, casual sip of his drink. "We make our own prisons, I think." And then he added offhandedly, "So your husband is a jealous man?"

The question took her off-guard. Was he jealous? That would imply a strong interest in what she did. There were portions of their lives that neither of the other ever entered — nor made an attempt to do so. Although she may have tried long ago, somewhere along the way, she gave up trying. It was too much effort. And her, she was as guilty as his indifference. She did not try to bring him to the earthly planes where she had spent most of her life. Truth be told, he would be like an alien attempting to navigate an unfamiliar landscape.

"I'm sorry. Was that question too personal?" he asked.

"I guess I'm just trying to figure out how to answer it. Yes and no, I suppose."

"Ah, very diplomatic and ambiguous, Annabelle." How comfortable he seemed now using her name as if it belonged to him.

"I suppose he's only jealous in the respect that he considers me an acquisition like an expensive car, a house — something that once bought should stay put until he requires something from it."

His dark eyes seemed to envelop her. "I see."

She was a bit shocked at herself for making such an admission to someone she barely knew. "I'm sorry. Maybe I shouldn't have said that."

"Sometimes it's easier to divulge personal truths to people who aren't a real part of your life."

"Maybe."

Maybe it was the drink going to her head, the strange mellowing mood of the darkened lounge. But it was unforgivable, divulging such personal matters to a stranger, a handsome, compelling, kind stranger who was saying all the right things.

She sighed deeply, "I really should go."

"Before you say too much?"

"I'm just in an odd mood tonight. My life isn't that bad."

She took another sip of her drink although she knew she shouldn't, and she continued talking although she knew it was ill-advised. "I don't know if I would call my life settling. I have a lovely home and friends, and I am financially secure. And my husband is a good man."

"Will you tell him about this?"

"This?" she asked with confusion.

"Will you tell him about having a drink with me?"

She hesitated. Two options— she could cover and say something that might stem the conversation or she could continue telling the truth and see where it leads.

"No, probably not."

He smiled seeming oddly gratified at her admission. "And why is that Annabelle, if he is not a jealous man?"

"He," she faltered. "He wouldn't understand. I don't share a lot with him."

He nodded as though he expected this response from her. "It's a pity not being able to share everything with the one person in the world you are pledged to be closest to."

"Marriage is different things to different people. Are you married, Gerard?"

He didn't answer immediately as though he were considering his choice of words. "No, not now, Annabelle, and if I were, I would hope I wouldn't be here with you."

She didn't know what she was expecting, but this jolted her and made her feel defensive. "I suppose that means that you feel you are a better person than I am."

He frowned, putting his brandy glass softly on the table. "I apologize. You mistake my meaning. I'm a traveler, and I have lived and seen much. For me to be married, that union would have to be all-encompassing. I would know my wife, my mate completely. Not just the parts I wanted to know, not just the parts of her I was comfortable with, but all of her. And that I believe shouldn't leave me time to entertain the company of other beautiful, mysterious women."

It was so strange listening to his voice, feeling nearly mesmerized by him and his thoughts. In some ways it was profoundly disturbing but so different, exotic, compelling to continue. "I don't think that's possible what you describe. It feels like a fantasy, a dream, but nothing that fits in the real world."

"Because you have never experienced it, you don't believe it exists."

"I don't believe people are capable of that. They are too flawed."

And then he smiled strangely, almost sympathetically. "And you are very sad and disillusioned. Tell me, was this always the life you envisioned for yourself?"

Another question that made her search too deeply into dank, dusty corners of her psyche. "I don't know. I guess when I was young I dreamed of something else, some fairy tale. A prince who worshipped me."

He watched her quietly but intently. "And then you found there are no princes?"

She nodded in agreement. "Honestly, I think men are too selfish to make some woman their whole world."

"But women?" then he stopped.

"Women do it all the time. It is in their nature."

"But wouldn't it be something to find a man worthy of such sacrifices?"

"I told you it's a fantasy."

He nodded, "Yes, yes, you did. Another drink Annabelle?"

Another drink, then another text. It was confirmed she was on her own for the evening, a dangerous confirmation. They were drinking wine now. Gerard St. Clair had insisted, and she was debating once again how to put an end gracefully to their interlude together.

"So, how long do you plan to stay in New Orleans?" she inquired.

He looked a bit bemused at the question. She did have to admit it seemed rather superficial, considering the personal ground they'd already covered that evening. But he seemed willing to play along. "Well a few days perhaps. My plans are flexible. And you, how long are you and your husband staying at the Royal Orleans?"

She swallowed on a curiously dry throat. "Just the night, we'll leave mid-morning." And then his eyes seemed to harden a bit as though he were considering something as he stared at her. "What is it?" she asked. "You're making me nervous."

"I'm sorry. I was considering the fact that, in all likelihood, this will be our only night like this. And I was wondering how your life will be tomorrow."

It was an odd thing for him to say but then again their whole conversation had been anything but commonplace. "I try not to focus on the future too much. I just live every day as it comes."

"Every moment Annabelle?"

She nodded slowly in agreement. "Sometimes every moment."

Unexpectedly, he reached across the table and took her hand in his. It was strange. The touch of his flesh sent a chill through her but a peculiar spark as well. The things he had seen, the life he had lived — a feeling of freedom coursed from his skin and flesh into her.

"You know freedom begins in the mind Annabelle. First you decide you are free, then the cage opens."

She listened. She was hungry, so hungry for it.

"Come," he said standing up. "Let's take that walk."

She stood up as well not thinking whether she should. "Then what?" she asked.

"Moment by moment," he responded taking her hand in his.

The Lake

The lake was serene, soothing, tranquil — all the things she sought. It was just the end of March, beginning to get warm but not intolerably hot as she knew too well the summers could be in Louisiana.

"Bridget"

"Yes?"

"Is everything all right with the house?"

She was renting for a month from a friend's cousin for a minimal fee.

"Yes, it's perfect."

"Are you sure you won't be lonely on the lake all alone?"

"No, it's exactly what I want."

It wasn't a divorce, after all, just a break-up or a break-off of an engagement. It had only been a month, and it had only been a month until the wedding. In fact, on Tuesday she should be getting married. But she wasn't. Instead, she was ensconced here on the lake, alone in this lovely house.

The house was on a hill, and she liked to walk down early in the evening to its long pier, which stretched into the water. The bugs were intense, so she generously sprayed herself with repellant.

"Are you upset?"

"I don't think so."

"You must be numb."

"That must be it."

It was an odd feeling, not knowing where your life was going. She was in between jobs, living on savings. Joe had a travel business. She was supposed to continue working with him, but once the engagement was off, that ended as well.

She had a degree in business and a degree in education and hadn't a clue where she was headed except down this hill to the pier.

"Are you sure?"

"Yes, I am."

"What happened?"

"I woke up."

There were a lot of trees on the descent, masses of unidentifiable shrubbery that partially shrouded the road leading down to the lake.

"You could get a job as a tutor until you land a regular teaching position."

"Maybe."

"You could go back to school for another degree."

"I don't know."

"You have to make plans."

"Do I?"

She finally made it down to the edge of the water. It glistened with so many colors, but again, it was still so peaceful. She breathed in deeply. Was she depressed? It didn't seem so. Numb? Maybe, but not with upset. Disconnected? Yes.

She rarely thought about Joe now, although they had been together for nearly three years. He'd wanted her to move in with him, but she'd resisted that.

She heard the sounds of the forest around her swelling and tried to feel anything. It hurt along the fringes, like nerves that had been dead and were slowly getting some sensation back.

Yes, perhaps it had been numbness, numb within her life.

She stood on the edge of the lonely pier and stared blankly at the beauty around her.

Then she heard the motor of an approaching boat, and she dimly registered that it was slowing down.

"I can't go through with this."

He was at his desk, completely absorbed in his laptop. "With what, honey?"

"With this, the marriage."

That had done it, finally got his attention. "Is this a joke?" he'd said. He was shocked. She could see it. He had everything he wanted and was satisfied. She wondered dimly how someone else could be so satisfied if she was so dissatisfied.

Different thresholds of expectations. Someone had said that, maybe her friend Susannah.

"You know life isn't all romance. Relationships are hard work, and they change and settle down," her mother's advice.

Perhaps they'd settled down into apathy, she mused.

It was a small boat with one or two seats at most. But this afternoon, creeping into evening, it held one occupant—a tall man wearing a baseball cap.

"So you've rented the Sandburn place?"

"Sorry?" she called out from her perch on the pier's edge.

The boat was many yards away. She'd wholly expected it to pass her by with maybe a wave, but it seemed to be creeping closer. Evidently, he was maneuvering it that way.

"You're staying here?" he asked. Hard to see the details of his features yet, still too far away.

She nodded, feeling so odd at the awkwardness of the exchange. "For a month."

His head bobbed in acknowledgment. "Mind if I dock for a minute?"

She frowned. How strange.

What was the protocol for such a request? She was a city girl. "Okay," she replied, completely ill at ease. Did criminals usually approach upon a lake in a boat? Approach lonely females who feel disconnected from their lives?

He edged the boat right to the pier's edge and handed her a rope. She stood there holding it dumbly while he sprang rather nimbly out of the boat. Taking the rope smoothly out of her hands, he knotted the end to the edge of the pier.

Then he turned to her. He was a youngish man, maybe in his thirties or forties, with dark brown hair and a beard and mustache.

"Is this okay?" he asked.

Directness caught her off guard. "Um, I guess."

He smiled broadly. "You're not used to this water thing."

"I'm from New Orleans, ferries, and riverboats."

He nodded, holding out his hand. "I'm Lance Jessup. I have a camp down the lake."

"Then you live here?"

Another easy-going smile, "Sometimes, I'm a writer. So it's a good getaway when I need the isolation. So why are you here from the big city for a month?" And then he paused, waiting for her to fill in the gap.

"Bridget Oneil."

He nodded, "Bridget Oneil. Sounds like a name for a story."

She laughed, "Oh, do make it an adventurous one."

"Of course."

Her city sense was dulled. Never get too close to a stranger. But he didn't feel like a stranger. He felt like the lake, soothing, undemanding, easy-going.

On the lower porch, beneath the house, there was a swing where they sat quietly talking. "Do you come here a lot?" she asked.

"A few times a year when I'm in my reclusive phase." And then he'd added, "Is that why you're here?"

She shrugged, "Maybe. I guess I'm at a crossroads and needed life around me to stop its roar so I could think."

"Well, I can certainly relate to that, Bridget." He used her name easily and had started to do so as soon as she'd given it to him. "You know the Indians used to camp along this lake. It was mystical for them."

She smiled, "Really? Mystical in what way?"

He stared out strangely into the distance. "They felt there were spirits in the forest."

He didn't stay long. She watched with curiosity as his boat disappeared around the bend of the shore.

"There's one very good restaurant in town, the only seafood restaurant. Would you like to have dinner with me tomorrow?"

She hadn't really expected it — wasn't really expecting anything. She'd been "out of the game" for so long. He watched her closely for an endless moment during her indecisive silence. "Sorry, I guess that came out of the blue. But I wasn't expecting to run into someone out here who seems like a kindred spirit."

She smiled, feeling utterly embarrassed by her lack of finesse. "Okay, well, why not. It's not as though my schedule is full."

"About six, and I'll come up the front way this time."

"What did I do?"

"It's not about you."

"You're breaking off our engagement. How can it not be about me?"

"I just don't know who I am anymore."

"You're going to be my wife."

"That isn't enough."

Dreams, dreams, aspirations, hopes, desires — the pull for anything. Where had it all gone?

She'd become tired and listless. Was that true that it wasn't him?

It was more about who she was when she was with him.

She pulled the blinds open at night and felt the darkness around her press in. *"They felt there were spirits in the forest,"* he'd said.

She closed her eyes and let herself reach out around her.

"Why did you let me waste all this time?"

"Do you think it was a waste?"

"I wanted a family, a wife."

"What about what I wanted?"

"What did you want?"

Ghosts, ephemeral ghosts — haunting her. What did she want? It became so folded into what he wanted.

It was a thick, heavy darkness around the house. Is this what they felt? But she could feel it pulling at her, tugging at her to understand, to feel again.

"You're not being fair. Give me a chance to fix things."

She breathed deeply. "I can't. I don't have it in me."

"You're not being fair."

There was guilt. It had almost made her stay. It might have been easier to give in and just collapse further into herself.

But something made her push outward.

And then a wave of unbelievable sleepiness passed over her.

"What kind of books do you write?"

He looked at her a bit oddly from across the table. "You really want to know?"

"Is it a secret?"

He picked up a French fry and took a bite slowly. "Don't want to frighten you away."

"Try," she murmured unexpectedly, even to herself.

"Horror, paranormal, ghost stories."

She stared at him a bit blankly, "Like Stephen King?"

"At times."

"Wow, sounds cool."

He smiled, seemingly pleased. "Think so? Some women would take one look and run the other way."

"Sounds exciting to me. I would imagine this sleepy little town would be inspiring."

And then he eyed her strangely, "I don't know, Bridget. The most inspiring thing I've found here in a long time is you."

He'd picked her up at 6:00 PM on the dot. She'd dressed casually — slacks, a short-sleeved sweater, and him in khakis and an untucked light blue shirt. Now that he was not in his outdoor garb, she could get a more complete impression of him.

He was tall and nice-looking—not devastatingly hand-some, but interesting—and definitely better-looking than Joe. His manner was effortless and sophisticated, one she found ap-pealing.

The restaurant itself wasn't terribly far from the house. It was just down the main highway, quiet, and not crowded at all.

"So tell me what sends a city girl to crave this kind of iso-lation — must be a story there."

"Wow, you are direct. Most people I know beat around the bush forever before they get to the point."

"Sounds like a waste of time."

"Yeah, I guess it wastes a whole lot of time," she laughed.

"And is a bit evasive."

She looked directly into his eyes — green eyes that were sparkling but also something else. He wasn't going to be put off this time. She could feel it on her skin. "Well, my story isn't nearly as exciting as yours."

"You'd be surprised what seems mundane to some people might be a treasure trove to someone else."

She sipped her draft beer. The seafood platter and beer ri-valed similar food she'd had in New Orleans. "Well, the truth is, I guess I came here to sort things out," she hesitated.

"Yeah, I remember that. Stop the roar so you could think. And there's more to this, I can feel it. But you can tell me to butt out if you want."

She took a deep breath. Why was this so hard? Maybe because she didn't want to bring her old life here. Here, it was simpler. Here, she could be anyone she wanted. Not that other girl. "Okay, I broke off an engagement recently," she rambled out rather quickly.

He stared at her a bit oddly, "Really?"

"You see, it's changed everything now."

"No, no, it just fills in pieces."

She shrugged, "Actually, I should be on my honeymoon right now."

Again, with the speculative stare. "That's really something. I knew there was something very troubled about you like you'd been through a hurricane or something big. You just had that great, mysterious aura."

She took another sip of beer, "Yeah, real great. So basically, I'm trying to figure out what to do next. The slates been kind of wiped clean."

He stared at her intently, studying, and then slowly said, "No, not really. You still seem to be carrying it around with you, if you don't mind my saying." Then he added rather quickly, "But this is a great place to figure things out. And maybe wipe that slate."

She frowned. She felt a bit awkward now, like he'd seen inside her messy bedroom or something like that. "You think so?"

"Absolutely." She nodded, toying with her platter contemplatively. "Sorry," he murmured. "I pushed."

"No, no, it's just strange talking about it. I guess it's still kind of fresh. It wasn't, well, anything obvious. I just decided I didn't like where my life was headed. You know, wasn't looking forward to anything, even getting married. Sounds bizarre, I guess."

He was calmly watching her. He had compelling, intense green eyes. "It sounds like you made the right decision, Bridget."

"Well, not everyone thinks so, and of course, I'm the bad guy for calling things off."

"What you did took a lot of courage. Some people would take the road of least resistance and settle. I'm divorced. Take it from me. It's much worse after the marriage to find out you've gone the wrong way. I admire you for taking hold of the reins and changing direction."

She laughed abruptly, "Yes, but just now, I'm not sure I know where I'm leading the horses."

"That's okay. You don't always need to know. Sometimes you just need to take a pause to reassess." And then he smiled encouragingly at her. "Listen to the spirits in the trees."

She thought about saying something else but didn't. But the comment felt disturbing.

They sat on her swing after dinner, drinking coffee she'd brewed. Lance Jessup had driven her all around town after dinner, pointing out lovely scenery and significant points of interest. Strangely, his mood had changed somewhat after her disclosures, although not nearly in the way she'd expected. He was more somber and contemplative but, oddly, more interested. Interested in what she thought, her impressions, as though he keenly wanted to hear her talk and move closer somehow. Evidently, what she'd told him had opened a door between them.

"Are you working on a book now?" she asked, disturbing a long stretch of quiet as they both seemed to be relaxing at the moment.

"Beginning one," he answered. She had invited him in for coffee, surprising herself. As he'd pulled up into the long stretch of driveway in front of the rustic house, it occurred to her how much she was enjoying their conversation. And how long she'd lived outside that very simple pleasure. To say she and Joe didn't communicate well seemed like a vast understatement. They'd settled into a pattern of exchange, brisk, cogent, nothing particularly enjoyable. But this evening, it had been something different. It had been languorous, like a lovely winding mountain road that put you into an altered state — something indulgent and joyful. And when he brought her home on a very basic level, she realized she wasn't nearly ready for it to end.

And then he eyed her a bit intensely, a look she was beginning to become accustomed to. "I hope you don't mind. I'm contemplating using you as the basis of a character. I mean, a woman renting an isolated house on a lake."

"And the forests around her are haunted and filled with spirits."

"Yes," he said quietly.

"What happens to her?"

He shrugs, "She meets a mysterious stranger."

She nodded, "Who isn't what he seems."

"Maybe you should write it."

"I'm not that creative."

"I doubt that, Bridget. In fact, I'm sure you underestimate yourself."

She sighed, "Maybe, I don't know. I feel—" then she stopped. Was it wise to keep confiding in someone she really knew so little about?

"You feel, please continue."

"Am I going to see it in print?"

"Not if you don't want it."

"I was going to say I feel like I don't know myself at all. That I got sidetracked in someone else's life. Does that sound pathetic?"

"No, it sounds sad, and unfortunately, it's very easy to do, especially for sensitive souls. It's easy for them to feel inadequate, and believe me, there are plenty of people out there ready to tell them that they are."

"Sounds like experience?"

"I've had my moments." She sipped her coffee silently, considering. "You know, at some point, it is important to understand the past, but on another level, you have to make peace with it and yourself."

She frowned, "Peace, how in the world do I do that?"

"Forgive yourself for whatever you think needs forgiving, and then let go."

She stared outside into the darkness of the night across the lake. A few distant lights twinkled, but for the most part, the only illumination was the moonlight stretching across the serene surface of the water. Lance Jessup had left some time ago, and she felt strangely torn by his unexpected presence in her life.

Part of her accepted the shroud of guilt that some insisted she wear as the author of disruption and dissatisfaction in so many lives. It astounded her how free and confident so many felt laying their own judgment on something that didn't even concern them. She was more than sure "those" people in question would scoff and hiss at the idea of her obtaining any measure of happiness, small as it might be so soon or ever for that matter.

And then there was the other side. As she stared into the night, she could feel herself walking out of the shadow of that thought pattern. She'd become empowered by leaving behind a life she didn't want. Like a snake shedding its skin and turning into something that might look the same on the surface but in an integral molecular sort of way was changed, transformed.

She slid open the sliding glass door and stepped onto the house's upper deck. The wood creaked beneath her sandals as she walked to the edge. She breathed deeply in the night air and felt as though perhaps she was shedding one more thing, one more thing from within — any concern now for the past or the future. It was an open book now, and she would follow the guide of a mightier hand than her own.

Her eyes slowly focused on the strange glow she noticed at a distance in the dark forest. She felt riveted to the spot as she saw it begin to move closer, like a soft, candescent, gossamer fabric of silk floating from the mass of trees nearer to the house. "The forest is filled with spirits," he had said. She was frozen not with fear but with mesmerizing anticipation.

His hands hesitated on the keyboard as he heard soft footsteps behind him. "Sorry," she whispered, "am I interrupting?"

He smiled to himself as he felt familiar hands lightly touch his shoulders.

He laughed softly, "You wouldn't believe what I'm doing. I've finally picked up that novel again, the one I started when we first met."

"The one about the house on the lake?"

"The one about you," he said lightly. "I think I'm finally ready to write it."

He picked up one of her hands and brought it to his lips — the hand that had worn his wedding ring for the past three years. "Is it getting scary yet?" she whispered in his ear.

"Just about to my love."

The Most Unlikely of Places

"Wherein there is no question of how we must meander forth into a treacherous world, though a world of our own making, which God himself still waits upon us to reform. Not in our image but in humility, charity, and perhaps forgiveness for our fellowman. Not in the wickedness of destruction but in the glory of creation. Although our God waits for us at the holy hour, it has always been our choice how we come to him, how we care and culture this land that he has gifted us with."

Then he hesitated, "There is still time for a new world to begin."

She took a sharp breath inward. Like a physical stab just between her ribs, she could tangibly feel his pain. His eyes rose from his prepared works on the podium as he began to search the congregation in the small church. She shivered inwardly because it felt as though he had begun to hunt for her. But she stepped backward internally, slightly hunching her shoulders, and in some regards, shrinking herself physically so she would blend in. She willed herself to be inconspicuous as her long gray woolen skirt swished nervously against those sitting on either side of her in the rustic wooden pews. Once the sermon concluded, she could easily withdraw. Much as she longed to stay, it would not behoove her to be discovered.

"Good citizens," he continued. "All we can do is persevere in these catastrophic days. Hold on to what is most godly, what is best in life."

She stilled her anxiety, unequivocally mesmerized by the sound of his voice. Yes, all she could do was hold on.

Once she was outside the church and away from other members of the congregation, she closed her eyes, using her tremendous power of focus, and slowly reopened them. It happened quickly, so quickly that she scarcely felt the journey. Around her were the familiar walls of her bedroom again within her apartment. The year was 2020, April 2020, and she was observing stay-at-home orders amidst the COVID-19 pandemic.

"*CeCe,*" it was scarcely a whisper in her mind. But she was accustomed to paying attention to whispers. She closed her eyes, putting her psyche in a receiving disposition. The soft image of her older sister, Amelia, floated into her inner vision.

"*Millie,*" she sent outward with a direct thought.

"*Where have you been? I've been trying to reach out to you for hours.*"

"*Hours?*" she sent back quizzically.

"*Well, an hour, I tried an hour ago and then just now.*" Amelia did tend to lean toward the dramatic side of things.

"*Sorry, I've been busy.*"

She could clearly see Amelia's face in her mind's eye. She lived up in Maine with her husband of two years and a toddler. It was a wonder she had time to do anything, much less play big sister to her. "*You know Mom is worried about you.*"

Her parents had also relocated up north, not so very far from Amelia's rural country house. Of course, this was the era of social distancing, but she suspected they snuck over to see her occasionally.

"*Why isn't she doing the checking-in then?*"

"*She's too sensitive. Her empathic abilities make her vulnerable to all the strong emotions around.*"

"*Well, you can tell her I'm fine. I'm only out at the grocery once in a while and as little as possible.*"

The vision of Amelia in her mind looked at her oddly, with skepticism, wrinkling her nose the way she always did, well, when she was in the flesh and in a snit.

"*You know Cecilia, it's not safe right now to travel too much.*"

"*I just told you —*"

"*That's not what I mean. There are things about, people about, capitalizing on all this upset. You — well, we really — have to be careful now more than ever.*"

A slight but substantial chill crept up her spine as she wondered exactly how closely Amelia was keeping tabs on her.

"*I'm aware,*" she mumbled, or as much as a mumble that could be achieved in thought transference.

"Stay safe."

"Always."

It was undisputable, however, that she did feel a somewhat desperate need to escape, not just from the four walls of each room of her one-bedroom apartment but from so much more.

"What does it feel like?"

"Panic, embedded deeper than the surface of my skin."

Her dad nodded with understanding in his remarkably green eyes. That was what she'd always noticed about him. No matter how snowy he got on the top, those eyes were always a brilliant emerald green.

"In some ways, you seem even more sensitive than your mother, Cecilia. And that's saying a lot. For your peace of mind, you'll need to learn to erect some armor and simply get away from the madding crowd occasionally. You just absorb too much."

Yes, indeed, she had been diagnosed as an intense empath by her family at a fairly young age. And here she was, trapped, away from her extended family during a pandemic. The very walls of her apartment building were oozing with anxiety and, in some regards, the sheer fear of its occupants.

Who could blame her for occasionally escaping the excruciating pressure, even if it was to the most unlikely of places?

"Reverend Bradshaw, we are so blessed to have you amongst us in these most trying of times."

He smiled at the elderly parishioner, Goody Burroughs, and was moved by her sincerity. Only six months earlier, he had stumbled onto this relatively obscure Puritan village of Saybrook in Connecticut. With a reasonable cover story, they had wholly embraced him more quickly than he'd ever expected. And he stayed, finding his rather unorthodox approach subtly melding into their dogma. But the truth was this area was ripe for his interference. It was weary, weary of its own inflexibility, weary of tearing itself apart with suspicion, weary of torturing and, at times, yes, hanging innocent people for witchcraft. In a nutshell, these people were feeling the weight of their misdeeds, and he was just the man to push them along that new path of enlightenment, albeit ever so gently, ever so gradually. He could be patient as he, too, was weary.

"My great niece Anne Greenwood was quite taken with your sermon as well."

"Anne?" he questioned, not having heard that name bandied about before in the village.

"Yes, the child arrived from the Roxbury colony of Massachusetts some weeks back."

"Some weeks back, Goody Burroughs?" he questioned, probing her resolve somewhat, but as he did, a look of confusion dropped across her pinched and wrinkled face and then a blank stare. Clearly, he surmised, there was nothing cohesive there in terms of memory. "Oh yes, I remember now, young Anne, a dark-haired girl." That was the only coherent fact he drew from this mishmash of flimsy threads in the old lady's recollections.

"Yes, Reverend Bradshaw, I felt sure I'd introduced you to her."

He smiled in a comforting manner. "I'm most certain you have. It is just my fatigue of late that may have caused my forgetfulness. Perhaps I will visit your farm soon and be reintroduced."

The lady smiled now, feeling more comfortable and complacent in the facade that had been perpetrated on her.

"Thank you, Sir. That would be most welcome," she murmured before she took her leave.

He leaned back into the rather uncomfortable chair near his stark wooden desk. That was the way of things here, stark, colorless, shredded of luxury. But on the other hand, it was quiet, true, devoid of pretension for the most part — except for the old ways he was working hard to purge them of.

So, all of that now could be disrupted by an interloper with selfish intent. It was true. He had felt something during the sermon, powerful energy. And he had now secured a concrete image of Anne Greenwood in his mind.

He could see it now in great detail and focused acutely on it. It was odd. The energy from her was faint. It appeared as though she had already moved on.

He could track her, but what would be the point if she was just passing through. There was more than the possibility that he could call on Goody Burroughs at her farm, and she would have no memory of her great niece visiting from Roxbury. The delicate illusion may have already begun to fade. Perhaps truly, there was nothing to do, no harm done unless, of course, she decided to return.

Cecilia roamed the apartment, attempting to calm her nerves. It should be a last resort, only when she absolutely needed to escape. This she told herself, repeatedly. And the idea of returning to the same place, well, that was just foolhardy. The way she ended up there in that little Puritan village was really quite random. She'd felt reckless, and instead of methodically planning out a voyage, as had been the way she'd been taught, she simply jumped in, allowing the currents of energy to bring her *somewhere interesting*. Imagine her surprise when she landed in the Puritan village of Saybrook in upstate Connecticut just before a church service.

She, of course, had the option of just being an observer and simply viewing. But, the strong comfort and familial feel that emanated from the crowd made Cecilia want to be a little nearer. She was hungry, emotionally hungry to feel closer to these people, who had different thoughts and emotions, not the same ones she'd felt herself drowning in day in and day out for so long. So, she stepped in, mentally donning the proper garb and, with a quick manifestation, attaching herself to a kind elderly couple. There didn't seem to be any harm. That was until she heard the booming voice from the pulpit — the young reverend that the town was half in love with.

And unfortunately, she knew why. He was magnetizing, mesmerizing, good-looking, and clearly, at least to her, not what he pretended to be. She sat solemnly with the congregation, head mostly bent and listened, listened to his words, his hypnotic words.

He was leading these people, hypnotizing them in some regard to do good. It was quite something. So much power, and he was using it to just set these people on a kind, selfless path.

But then, in the middle of everything, something curious happened. He paused, staring into the small crowd with those piercing blue eyes, and she knew he was looking for her.

Lucky for her, she had been able to throw her energy signature off in another direction so that he was confused. And then, of course, she quickly departed once the service was finished. But it was disappointing. She had been looking forward to seeing Goody Burroughs's farm and spending the afternoon with her family. But there wasn't enough time, and it was too dangerous to return. Perhaps she shouldn't have gone at all. Perhaps.

Time was a construct. Once he accepted this fully, everything else became simpler.

He walked into the autumn forest outside the small village of Saybrook. You could smell burning leaves somewhere, but the source was unknown. Elias Bradshaw had already begun to focus and move through the layers.

When all came to fruition, he stood in the center of his den in his Ozark Mountain home in Missouri.

His head spun with dizziness, and he dropped to his knees. Distracted, he noted that his puritanical clothing had shifted, and he wore a white shirt and tan slacks, modern garb.

He had no idea what time frame it was. He'd been inexact, purely zeroing in on finding her. He hadn't intended it, but she had seeped into his consciousness, first as a curiosity, then progressively as an obsession. He had taken the time to ride his horse, Sanctuary, out to the Burroughs homestead. Joseph and his wife Esther seemed more than surprised at his unexpected visit. And without really inquiring, he noted that there was no niece by the name of Anne visiting, nor did any trace of her remain in the memory of any of the members of the Burroughs family, including the grown children or their young offspring. She had simply vanished as though she had not been.

Eli rose on shaky legs, making his way over to his computer. He'd been gone for months, so it would undoubtedly be occupied with updates for some time. He noted the date, however, April 16th, 2020. That was a bit later than he'd expected to return, but then again, his target, so to speak, had been inexact.

He settled into his padded leather office chair and manipulated the keyboard to the news before the machine became entangled in setting things right. His eyes widened a bit at the headlines — pandemic, lockdown, COVID-19.

What in the world had he missed?

"Are you OK?"

"Yeah."

"Are you getting enough to eat?"

"Yep."

"Have you been to the grocery?"

"Yes, a few days ago."

"Are you going early in the morning? Are you wearing a mask?"

"Yes, Mom," she could feel it deeply. Her mother's anxiety was actually soaking into her hand as she touched her cell phone. She wondered if she put her on speakerphone if it would be less impactful. "I'm fine. Just let me finish up my classes this semester, and I'll see if I can make it up near you."

There was silence on the line that was uncomfortably protracted. "CeCe, a lot of state borders are closed right now. You'd have to go into six weeks of quarantine."

"I know, Mom. It won't be like that forever. Give it time."

"But Cecilia, you are staying put. Aren't you darling?"

"Don't worry, Mom. Everything is fine."

He did a little research, learned the rules of the moment, moved some stocks around, ensured the autopay on all his bills was still working, and stocked up the pantry of his Ozark mountain home. He'd left here about nine months ago. So, he wasn't so very far out of touch. Except that it felt succinctly as though the whole world had changed while he was gone.

He knew he was on the same linear plateau as Goody Burroughs' great-niece but not geographically. Before he left the Saybrook village, he had been able with some difficulty to uncover some of the archived knowledge in Esther's brain. He had a strong image of Anne, a woman in her mid-20s, dark-haired, with large green eyes — and more than that her vibrant and complicated energy signature. She was south of him if he didn't miss his mark, somewhere in Louisiana.

Other impressions he absorbed were that she was sensitive, gifted, shy, emotionally needy, and sharply intelligent. And the question became why he was so intent on pursuing her when there was unfinished business in so many other places.

That, he didn't know. But since Eli had committed, he could either go to her—he hesitated, considering that option for a moment—or bring her here. It wouldn't exactly be kidnapping, just purposefully sidelining a voyage.

The old woman looked confused. "My dear, I thought you'd left, gone back to Roxbury."

Cecilia smiled warmly at Goody Burroughs. It had been too confused, the return. She'd intended to take a brisk walk outside the farm, with no detection, just to breathe in the fresh air and get away from the adversity that was the city of New Orleans in April of 2020.

So many people were shut in, upset, angry, and lost as they felt their way of life had been peeled away from their clutching fingertips. It was far too much pain and high emotion for her to filter out. And there was simply no place, no place she could go to escape it — no place she knew that was in her timeline. But here, maybe just for an instant, she could be free.

"Please go inside Esther, and forget me," she murmured. She was somewhat surprised that her presence had stirred up the tangle of memories she'd planted in the old woman. Truly, by now, she'd felt that she would have been simply forgotten.

The elderly woman seemed confused as she hesitantly turned about and headed back toward the house, as Cecilia had requested.

Her father had taught her the finer points of hypnotism with the voice and transference of thought.

She turned, heading back to the forest. It was clear she couldn't stay. It wasn't fair, tampering with these good people. And there was the risk that sooner or later, they might put things together, even manage to catch her and put her in the stocks or drown her or whatever they used to do to witches in those days. She focused as she walked back towards the woods with a heavy heart. There was no help for it — no place else for her to go.

The swirl came quickly, but she stabilized her inner core as she traveled and heard the high rush of the storm in her ears. When things began solidifying around her, she felt the wetness on her cheeks. She hadn't even realized she'd been crying.

But as the blurriness of her eyes began to clear, something much more ominous became apparent to her. These walls, this furniture, this was not her apartment.

She took a sharp breath, recognizing she was in a rather large, rustically decorated den flanked by huge, picturesque windows. Now she truly couldn't breathe as fear took hold.

The voice, quite startlingly, came from behind her. "You must forgive me, Mistress Anne. But I found it rather imperative that we meet."

She stayed rooted to the spot, not wanting to or able to turn around at the moment. But that voice—it was unmistakable.

In only seconds, he walked around to stand in front of her. "Of course, if you had stayed put, you might have eluded me." He was now dressed in modern clothes, blue jeans, and a white button-down shirt, but his identity was unmistakable. "But I understand, from my own experience as well, that when you have a gift, it's difficult to allow it to lie dormant." She swallowed on a dry throat. Undeniably, it was Reverend Bradshaw, who she'd heard give a sermon just two days before in the Connecticut colony of Saybrook over 350 years ago.

He suspected there was a genetic component as it seemed to run in families — the ability to transfer one's physical form through different planes of reality, the easiest being currents of perceived time. But of course, as he'd learned, other possibilities also existed.

Anne, the name was false. This he knew well before the meeting. She was a young woman, in his estimation, in her mid-to late 20s, with mid-length dark brown hair, fair skin, green eyes, and fine bone structure. She was around 5 feet 6 inches, willowy, as his mother would describe her, and delicate. Everything about her felt delicate, which, of course, was at odds with the amount of raw psychic energy he felt flowing off of her in excess after her excursion.

She wasn't saying much, just staring at him with wide, guarded eyes. "I saw you preaching," finally, she spoke.

He frowned, "Giving a sermon, yes, but I didn't see you there, just later in Goody Burroughs's mind."

Again, there was silence, and then she answered with steel in her voice. "I wasn't there long."

"Why? Why were you there at all Miss—"

He searched, in fact, had to go deep because there were so many barriers to information within her. "Jamison."

She flinched. He'd hit a target. "Tell me. Do these extraordinary abilities run in your family?"

"What do you want?" she snapped out with evident apprehension. It was clear mentioning her family had hit a nerve.

That was a question. What did he want from her exactly? "The village of Saybrook is a personal project of mine. I don't want anyone interfering with what I'm doing there."

"I wasn't interfering," she murmured.

"Then why were you there — Cecilia?" Finally, he got it, and she didn't look at all happy about it.

"I was just looking for a place to get away for a while. There was no harm intended. I'm sorry if it seemed that way, Reverend Bradshaw."

The formality and the softness of her declaration caught him off guard. "Eli," he said with just a flickering of a smile. "Get away from what exactly Cecilia?"

She looked at him with more than a tinge of incredulity, "All the pain, of course."

She should be more afraid. He'd kidnapped her, and plucked her right out of the cosmos on her way home. But oddly, she wasn't. Something about him, something about this place — the energy was literally streaming inward from these huge windows, glass doors, directly from the mountains. It was so lovely, quite soothing. And as for Reverend Bradshaw, she couldn't help but remember how comforting and, in fact, nurturing he'd seemed to his congregation. Eli as he told her to call him — well, he was younger than she'd thought initially when he'd given the sermon at the rustic little church in Saybrook. Maybe he was in his 30s, early 30s, or mid, she thought — good-looking, on the slender side, tall, black hair, dark blue eyes, amazingly intense dark blue eyes.

Her mind told her succinctly that she should feel more threatened. There was no debate as to how vulnerable a position she was in. But all she felt in the moment was oddly intrigued.

"Why?" she muttered, stopping herself from elaborating on the question.

"Why, what exactly, Cecilia?"

"The village, the Puritans — what are you trying to do there?"

He seemed a little taken aback at the inquiry, drawing a pronounced breath before he spoke. "Trying to plant seeds, I suppose, help them evolve. These people have a concerning history — paranoia and superstition. I'm trying to push the needle a bit, draw them into a better way of thinking."

She considered for a moment, feeling. He was being truthful. She had a built-in barometer for such things. It sort of went hand in hand with being an empath. "Noble," she commented softly.

"Is that sarcasm, Miss Jamison?"

"No, I was being perfectly serious. It is noble, a worthy way to share your gifts."

He eyed her with curiosity. He didn't know quite what to make of her. She could feel it. Clearly, he shared her ability to travel but not her empathic skills. "Pain, you said."

She cleared her throat, realizing for perhaps the first time how awkward it was, both of them standing in this enormous room, ostensibly interrogating each other. "Yes, of course, the pandemic — I don't know if you've noticed, but people are losing it. The pain, fear, anxiety, and rage can be overwhelming. I live in a city. It's torturous to feel all of that almost round the clock. And I have to get away from it at times."

She felt dizzy. She had forgotten to eat, not smart, and her blood sugar tended to fall quite easily.

"Are you alright, Cecilia?"

She put her hand to her head. Perhaps also, it was more, entirely too much stress. "I—" she began but couldn't finish.

Then suddenly, she felt his hands on her arms, stabilizing her. He was concerned. How nice. "How can I help?" he whispered.

"Maybe something to drink."

Then his arms went around her waist as she stumbled.

He made her a cup of tea with slices of cheese, crackers, and cut-up apple pieces. And he had to admit, it seemed to be helping. The color was returning to her cheeks, not so pale now, and Cecilia Jamieson was not so furtive as she'd initially seemed. She was hardly the threat he had first anticipated. But then again, in his experience, threats didn't always come in the most obvious packages.

"You were taking quite a risk, you know. I don't mean because of me," he course-corrected. He wanted to redefine himself as someone supportive and kind in her mind.

Her wide eyes focused directly across the rustic, cedar wood dinette table to him. He felt something odd. In fact, he'd felt something odd every time she looked at him this way, which had actually been more than a number of times in their very short acquaintance.

He could feel it on his skin, within. Somehow, she was assessing him with a barometer he didn't understand. "What do you mean?" she asked flatly, then took another sip rather nonchalantly from the steaming mug of chamomile tea.

"Well, to start, the stories, fabrications you planted in Goody Burroughs's mind about her niece, weren't very substantial and would not have held up to close scrutiny. And, of course, were further undermined by your abrupt removal of them."

"As I said," she answered a bit dryly, "I didn't plan to stay long."

He nodded, "Yes, but you did return."

Her mouth pursed a bit. He was beginning to note that Cecilia did not tend to exhibit strong emotion, so one had to read the subtleties. At least, that was his experience of her in this very brief interlude. "Only temporarily, just near the forest. The energy there is very calming I found." And then she sighed, shaking her head in a way he found rather charming, "Though I did run into Goody Burroughs for a moment. I made sure I was thoroughly erased from her memory when I left, as I never intended to return. But then, of course, you intercepted me and brought me here on my way back."

He picked up a round sesame cracker and a slice of cheddar, shoving it in his mouth as he considered how to respond. "Just the back-and-forth nature of memories, placing them, then removing them, destabilizes them. You must understand, Cecilia. These people were hanging witches only a few years ago. It was a barbaric time. They were filled with fear, superstitions, and ostensibly paranoid about everything. Believe me, you wouldn't want to become something they perceived as a threat."

She looked down, piddling with a piece of cheese at her fingertips. "I am sorry, Eli. What you're talking about? I really didn't feel that sort of energy in Saybrook."

"Yes, I understand. The community is in the process of evolving. It's not unlike someone with an addiction who hits rock bottom. It is only at that point that there is the possibility for change. Unfortunately, that change is tenuous at best, and it is so easy to fall back into old patterns."

She nodded slowly, clearly considering what he'd said. "I hope I didn't disrupt things for you too much."

He hesitated. Her sincerity truly had caught him off-guard. "Believe me when I say my concern is largely for your well-being, Cecilia." As an awkward silence ensued, he leaned back in the wooden chair. He felt like a brute. It was clear that this woman was in legitimate distress. And then, in the moment, he did something that maybe was ill-advised, presumptuous, or 100 million other things. He leaned toward her a bit, over the small expanse of the round table, and put his hand over hers.

Initially, she flinched at the contact, and he could feel things through her skin, a calamitous amount of sensitivity. "You're an empath," he murmured with a degree of surprise.

"Yes," she answered softly, not pulling her hand away but adjusting it slightly.

"I still don't understand how a Puritan village could possibly feel calming to an empath."

Her eyes snapped up, looking into his face with questions. "It is unpredictable, but you seem quite drawn and invested in the place yourself, Reverend Bradshaw."

There was an edge in her voice. An edge, he found, he actually quite liked. The kitten evidently had claws. She had surprised him, but then again, given what she'd done and was capable of, he shouldn't have been all that surprised.

"Touché," he murmured. "There is something about the area, even the people there, that transcends their violent history."

"Yes, things clearly aren't always so obvious on the surface."

He exhaled sharply. "You're speaking of yourself," and at that moment, she withdrew her hand.

"Why am I here again?" her voice was curiously emotionless, as though the answer were just of peripheral interest to her.

"I wanted to make sure you weren't a threat."

She nodded, "And now that we've chatted, Reverend Bradshaw. Do you think I am?"

He couldn't be sure, but he almost felt she was teasing him using the moniker of reverend. "I'm assessing Miss Jamieson."

She sighed lightly, looking at him oddly. She was not threatened, he thought, though he couldn't be sure. He was definitely no empath and not very skilled in reading others' emotions. "I believe you but am not sure what you're assessing. So, why don't we stop dancing, and you tell me what you'd really like to know."

She could leave. CeCe realized this early on in their conversation. There was literally nothing and no one holding her here in Elias Bradshaw's curious mountain abode.

But the odd truth was that she didn't want to leave, not yet. It was soothing here. The energy was lovely, and it was far enough away from the madding crowd that she didn't feel claustrophobically torn apart by all the angst and upset encompassing the current pandemic siege. In a nutshell, she could breathe here, so she wasn't in that much of a hurry.

And Eli, well, regardless of how formidable he'd initially presented himself, he was pretty easy on the eyes and on the psychic senses.

Not unlike his house, in some inexplicable way, she found him soothing as well.

He strummed his fingers on the dinette table for a moment, not answering. Perhaps he was frowning a bit, but it made her smile. "You know, I really have no agenda here, Eli," she paused, allowing herself to consider how well she liked the sound of his name on her lips, she definitely liked it better than Reverend Bradshaw. "I'm not a threat to — well — whatever you felt you were accomplishing with the people of the Saybrook village." She shrugged, "Honestly, I was just looking for an interlude where I could relax. It gets difficult." She hesitated, wondering with concern just how much she needed to confide. "I feel too much, feel it like it's my upset, my pain, and I really can't do anything about it. You know, personal paths and all."

She focused on his face and realized he was staring at her intensely. "I see that," he said quietly.

"So, I guess I can go then and leave you to your machinations."

"Machinations," he softly echoed with some question in his voice.

She nodded, just a bit. "Yeah, but I don't mean it in a diabolical way. I mean, I'm certainly not looking to interfere. I just wanted a bit of fresh air. That was all, really."

His hand had ceased strumming, but he still considered her intently. "So, your family, are they?" then he stopped.

There was a bit of a silent gap, so she nervously filled in. "Like me? A bit, I mean they could hop around if they wanted to, but they keep it rather low-key. But not the other stuff—"

"Empathic abilities."

"Right, they all have their strengths but mine, well, it's needless to say it's always seemed like a bit of a deficit in the big picture."

"Why would you say that?" he said quietly.

"I mean, honestly, what do I do with it? Seems like I'm spending most of my time just stemming the bleeding — I mean the upset."

"Feeling others' emotions? It's a powerful gift. Seems as though it could be extremely valuable."

She took a breath, glancing away. He was way too intense. It made her feel a myriad of things all at once. She wasn't used to people studying her so closely. "How about your family?"

"My family?"

She looked up at the sort of blank stare on his face. "Yes, are they gifted like you?"

Then, there was a gulf of hesitation for such an innocuous question. After all, he had asked her. "No, I mean I have no idea. I was adopted."

Now, this did take a moment to sink in. "Adopted, really?" His admission stunned her in a way. "So, you had to figure all this out on your own."

"Yes, in most respects."

"Wow," she said softly, feeling legitimately impacted in a way she really couldn't sort out at the moment. She looked down to see if he was still holding her hand but was surprised to see that he wasn't. Because it felt undeniably as though he had been.

He hadn't actually asked her what he really wanted to know because he wasn't sure himself. Instead, he had let her go, rather let her leave, but kept tabs, as was his way, on exactly where she had gone. Just in case there was a need, Eli told himself. No, he did not truly consider her a threat. He had run across only a handful of others in his time, navigators as he liked to call them. And some he would indeed designate self-interested and others, anarchists of a type, promoting discord, and chaos. But Cecilia Jamison, no, was undeniably not one of these.

"It must have been terribly difficult for you. Your birth family, could you ever find them?"

He'd been surprised that she was so interested. "They're dead. I was an orphan. It was a storm."

She sort of slumped in her chair as though there was a genuine impact to his words, maybe the empathic thing. "Oh, how horrible."

"I was a baby, so I wasn't attached to anyone," he said flatly.

He could feel her doing something, maybe opening up, checking if he was being truthful, perhaps even checking for pain. He didn't know for sure. He'd had little experience with genuine compassion.

"I couldn't imagine not having my family," she murmured. "They help keep me sane."

"And yet, you still feel the need to escape."

She hesitated, clearly struck by and weighing his statement. "They're up north, near my sister. I elected to stay behind and finish some schooling. I didn't expect to be trapped in a pandemic."

"I'm sure no one did," he murmured.

She sighed, and he could feel despondence in that sigh, though he was not an empath, so he couldn't be sure. "Yes, seems so, and most don't have the option to escape."

"Nor the extreme sensitivity to other people's pain as you do."

She looked at him intensely, engaging his gaze directly. She was beautiful, but it was mostly that glow that she seemed to exude. "I don't know about that. I've always thought there are more people out there like me, but maybe they just don't realize it." Then she slightly frowned, and he knew what was coming as though it were plastered somewhere on a giant billboard. "I need to get back Eli."

"Of course," he said softly, realizing somewhat surprisingly that deep down, he really didn't want to let her go.

He spent the next week in Connecticut. After taking care of immediate business in his Ozark home in Missouri, he left, quite determined to keep his focus on keeping the small battleground village of Saybrook on the right path, sowing seeds of humanity and generosity amongst his traditionally inflexible flock. And there were signs of progress, slow as it might be, and he felt gratified in his efforts except — except that some distant unacknowledged seed had also been sown in him. He felt, actually, somewhat alone. Now that he'd had a brief brush with a kindred spirit, he felt oddly restless and incomplete.

As he gave his sermon on Sunday, he looked out amongst the Saybrook congregation and glimpsed Goody Burroughs and her husband. He didn't have to ask her to be certain she had no memory of her niece Anne from the wilds of Massachusetts.

But the problem was that he did remember her. Her face was now clearly etched in his mind.

When he prepared to leave, he bookmarked the precise time to easily pick up where he left off. Although in truth, he had no idea when he would return.

Cecilia dreamed that she walked barefoot through the French Quarter. The city was couched in darkness save for the streetlamps, but unfortunately, she had to dodge huge chunks of broken glass on the sidewalk.

"*It's representational.*" She could hear her father's voice distinctly in her mind.

She felt the pain of the punctures on the soles of her feet. It was clear she could not avoid all the damage.

"*Don't fight it so much, Cecilia. Let it be what it is. You cannot hold yourself apart and be untouched by the pain that is around you.*"

"It feels like I will drown in it," she muttered.

"*You won't. Accept it. You are stronger than you think.*"

She spent the early morning and much of the afternoon focusing on school. Two major research papers were due at the end of the week, which she'd spent more than a bit of time ignoring. But despite what she was battling in her mind and on her skin, she dug in deep, working on erecting significant enough mental barriers so that she could focus.

By early afternoon, she felt exhausted but also oddly restless. Maybe a drive, or she had some school friends she could zoom with, but she'd been so reclusive the last month that she had no idea how receptive they might be to her.

Then, unexpectedly, there was a substantial quick knock on her front door. In fact, two sharp knocks, then they stopped. Maybe a package? But no, those usually came through the front office. She approached the door suspiciously, a mask she'd picked up from a small table nearby firmly perched on her face. Then momentarily, she let those barriers she worked so hard to erect that morning slip just a notch so that she might see.

The realization felt like a jolt. It simply couldn't be. But a bit aggressively, she pulled the door open wide. "Eli," she murmured with surprise, recognizing him instantly, though he was similarly disguised in his black mask.

"Cecilia," he said lightly, "hope I haven't caught you at a bad time."

She frowned a bit in confusion, though, of course, he couldn't see that. He looked casual, in fact even more casual than the last time she'd seen him. He wore just a t-shirt and blue jeans with tennis shoes — not at all the sharp, unrelenting Reverend Bradshaw or even that other aggressive, determined man he'd been at his house in the Ozarks.

"No, my schedule is pretty wide open just now. Do you want to come in?"

He nodded, and she felt something tug at her heart a bit. Oh dear, was she getting a crush? "Yes, that would be great."

The apartment wasn't very big but filled with light—in fact, cream-colored woods everywhere—coffee tables, end tables, rocking chairs, and bookshelves. It had the feel of something one might see near the beach. In addition, on the walls were paintings with muted colors of mountain and seaside scenes.

"Do you paint?" He asked. He'd followed her lead and divested himself of the mask once he was inside. Evidently, she didn't consider someone who'd spent the balance of their time at a Puritan village a high risk for spreading the Covid infection.

"Yes, I dabble." Of course, it could have been anyone's work, but he just had a feeling. He leaned in taking a closer look, soft colors but such precision in the images.

"Looks like more than dabbling, they're very good," he murmured.

"Would you like some tea?" she was just beside him, waiting quietly. Clearly, she hadn't been expecting guests. She was wearing an oversized, purple button-down shirt and white shorts. But then again, why would she? They were amid a pandemic.

He turned around. There she was, waiting quietly for an answer. "I suppose you're surprised to see me here."

Her arms were crossed in front of her, hair pulled back loosely in a bun. And he was drawn, couldn't help it, couldn't deny it. That was the crux of the matter. "A bit, I mean, I thought you were satisfied I wouldn't be causing you any problems."

"Well, there are problems, and then there are problems."

"Meaning what exactly?" she asked, squinching her brows together ever so slightly in a very endearing way.

"Tea would be great, Cecilia."

She nodded, "My family calls me CeCe."

"But Cecilia is such a lovely name."

She smiled a bit, clearly appreciating the overblown compliment. "I'll put on the kettle," she answered, then disappeared through a door that he surmised led to the kitchen.

He settled down on the light blue striped loveseat. They were in the middle of a city, but this room felt like the ocean. And yet, she struggled to find peace here. She must be very sensitive indeed.

They drank tea in her light, airy den, and Eli seemed markedly more relaxed than when he kidnapped her earlier in the week and brought her to his mountainside abode. Now he was all pleasantries which puzzled her and intrigued her simultaneously. She noted that on paper, it certainly did have all the ingredients for the beginning of a spicy romance novel, but he was notably all business in most respects.

"I do have to admit I was surprised to find you on my doorstep. I don't know if you've heard, but we're in a lockdown, and anyway, I thought you spend your free time ensuring that the people of Saybrook stay on the straight and narrow."

He smiled, undaunted, it seemed, by her pointed comments. "I did spend much of the week there. But I am honestly feeling satisfied that my time there is ending. They are in a better place, and I've sowed enough seeds to feel satisfied that they will continue that way." He sipped his tea somewhat pensively, filling her with the impression that his answer was well thought out.

"So, that's what you do, plant seeds to help people find the right path."

He looked at her directly, and she felt a distinct jolt of connection. Her father called it a latent ability she had for prescience or future glimpsing. It wasn't a solid talent and rarely reared its head except in random, uncontrollable flashes.

But she did feel, right down to her bones, that she and Eli would mean much more to each other, and consequently, their futures were intertwined.

"At times, I've had the good fortune to study with mentors, those who showed me how to put my gifts to good use to aid humanity."

"People like us," she murmured with interest.

"Some, some with other gifts." He cleared his throat a bit, then said, "Have you ever considered using your gifts in such a way, Cecilia?"

"You mean other than for my comfort."

"I'd hardly call escaping an insufferable situation for your comfort, rather a necessity."

She smiled, "I think you're being kind."

"Well, I have to say that's not something I've been accused of too often."

"I don't know. I saw a lot of kindness in Reverend Bradshaw, even when he was giving his fiery speeches." She sipped her tea, a little embarrassed at her disclosure. She was in the rocking chair adjacent to the sofa where Eli was sitting. She deliberately hadn't wanted to be right next to him. He exuded an energy that unsettled her, not exactly bad, but disturbing at a level. "My family has always made more of an effort to blend in and suppress our oddities more than not. So, no, I'm just getting through college — not on an altruistic mission, so to speak."

Eli eyed her pensively again as though he were considering. "You have such gifts. They could come in handy."

"Handy for what exactly?"

"My next project, actually. I was wondering if you might consider coming with me."

A hesitation seemed to wrap around them, around the room, taking hold and filling up all the awkward space.

Then she spoke softly, incredulously, and he couldn't help it. It made him smile. "Go with you?"

Now, he sipped his tea. He hadn't intended this, hadn't intended to ask, hadn't really intended to come here.

He wasn't at all sure why he had. Loneliness was an easy answer but not exactly the correct answer. It had begun when he first sensed her in Saybrook during the sermon. When he first glimpsed her in Goody Burroughs mind, the mysterious Anne grew incrementally, first as an interest, a fascination, then taking radical hold and in truth bordering on an obsession.

Then, when they finally met, talking at his home in the Ozarks, and she'd left, it almost felt like a vacuum. It felt tangible, as though a bright, vibrant light that had been absent from his life was suddenly taken away. And he missed it.

"Does that sound preposterous to you?"

Her face looked a little blank, a little confused. "I don't know. I don't really know what you have in mind."

He took another sip of his tea just to fill time. It wasn't as hot anymore, and he wondered if he'd made a disastrous mistake jumping into this. "I can see why you'd say that."

And then several tangible beats of silence. "You don't know, do you?"

"What's that?" he muttered.

"You haven't a plan, do you? Not a clue what you mean."

"Well," he sighed, carefully placing the tea mug on the ceramic coaster in front of him. He was prodigiously exacting how he set it because he didn't want to meet her eyes. This was painfully awkward. "No, no, I agree. I haven't a clue. It just feels, well—"

"I know," she said softly.

Then he did meet her eyes. "You do?"

"I— well — I felt something when I heard you speak as Reverend Bradshaw and all that. I just felt this energy— this pull," she tacked on quietly.

He nodded slowly, "Yes, yes, that's it, a pull. Is that why—" Then he stopped, the semi-question hanging in the air.

"Yes, why I came back to Saybrook."

He just stared at her in amazement. She was so lovely and possibly slightly blushing, but he couldn't be sure. "It's probably why I intercepted you as well."

"You said you thought I might be a threat."

He cleared his throat, "Well, you might have been — I suppose. But I was curious. I hope I didn't upset you too much."

"No," she sighed deeply. "I mean, I have been agitated, mostly because of how things are, the people around — so many violent, raw emotions. It's draining, hard to shut out."

"Not as much at my house."

Her eyes widened a bit. They were lovely large green orbs filled with depth and light. "Your house?"

"I mean the energy. It's more remote, not so many people dealing with their anxiety."

She nodded slowly, "I suppose."

"So, maybe you could spend some time there and rest, relax, and we could figure things out."

"I— I have my studies to finish."

He smiled slightly, really liking this idea. "Bring them. I have Wi-Fi. I'll give you all the space you need. And I'll cook dinner."

She looked at him with curiosity, perhaps warming to the idea. "You cook?"

"I do, often, though I'm a bit out of practice. There was a housekeeper back in Saybrook. She cooked hearty meals."

"I would imagine."

"So, will you come with me?"

"When?" she murmured.

"How about now, and we'll make it up as we go along."

She laughed softly, and he felt hope and optimism in his skin. "Sounds creative."

"Yes, I imagine it will be."

The Lady in the Blue Dress
6 x 9 Softcover & Hardcover 214 pages
ISBN 978-1-61342-600-5
ISBN (Hardcover) 978-1-61342-418-6

When she was a child, Mika Devalieur was introduced to her grandmother's most precious possession — a priceless and mysterious painting that she simply called The Lady in the Blue Dress. Upon Adele St. Clair's death, the painting is left in the care of her granddaughter with only one stipulation. Mika must hand over the family heirloom to a total stranger. Mika Devalieur desperately wants to deny her beloved grandmother's last request, but she can't. Torn between her Gran's last wishes and her desire to hold onto the Lady, she ultimately journeys to rural Virginia, where an enigmatic man shows her that this painting is only the beginning.

What quickly becomes clear is that James Clairmont knows much more about her and the Lady than he is letting on. He begins to slowly unravel a powerful supernatural connection that spans three generations of her family. Mika finds herself desperate to uncover the entire truth before she falls in love with a man filled with so many secrets — secrets about him, about her, and most especially about The Lady in the Blue Dress. (First published on Kindle Vella, episodes 1-23.)

Dumaine Street
6 x 9 Softcover & Hardcover 306 pages
ISBN 978-1-61342-902-0
ISBN (Hardcover) 978-1-61342-416-2

Voices in her head, catastrophic emotions, hallucinations — Rebecca Wells is more than convinced that she is losing her mind. And as a last-ditch effort, she contacts a self-professed counselor who seems convinced he can help.

Gabriel Sutton has abandoned the world of medicine to navigate a realm filled with psychic phenomena. Diagnosing Becca with extreme empathic abilities, he struggles to help her stabilize her gifts while trying desperately not to fall in love with his patient.

From the realm of vulnerability into a crusade to use their profound gifts to rescue others from peril on the other side of death, these two follow an astonishing and unpredictable path into each other's hearts.

The Tethering
A Portent of Crows
6 x 9 Softcover & Hardcover 201 pages
ISBN 978-1-61342-599-2
ISBN (Hardcover) 978-1-61342-419-3

Deborah Brandt's beloved Aunt Gena always told her that she was special, a bit different, and would have to live her life, unlike other people. Of course, this she disregarded as the ramblings of her lovely but notably eccentric aunt. Although there were the things that Aunt Gena said that seemed true — like Deborah being sensitive to energy shifts, having potentially psychic impressions, and dreaming of a spirit guide — none of it could be real. But the most ridiculous thing that her Aunt Gena told her before she died was that someone special was out there for her. She said that he was an extraordinary man who was not only her perfect match but someone who she would learn from so that they could help the world in difficult times. How ridiculous! It sounds like a fairy tale, and no such person exists.

Daniel Wren is unique. He has been raised and trained from a young age to hone his psychic gifts. He lives in a world unimagined by most. And he has been waiting for years to contact his counterpart, soulmate, if you will. But the problem is that she is painfully unaware of the type of life that he lives and the life she would be entering into if they came together.

His dilemma becomes how best to proceed. How can he win her over and move forward before outside forces take that decision away from him?

Travels into the Breach
Accounts of a Reluctant Mystic
6 x 9 Softcover & Hardcover 171 pages
ISBN 978-1-61342-323-3
ISBN (Hardcover) 978-1-61342-417-9

At first glance, his life seems quiet, serene, and even uneventful. Malachi McKellan, a 65-year-old widower and author of esoteric books, lives largely as a recluse in a house situated just off the banks of Bayou St. John in New Orleans. But unbeknownst to most, he is also a bit of a detective, a specific kind of detective whose specialty is psychic attacks. Alongside his lifelong companion and spirit guide Simon Tull, a 19th-century, 20-something English gent, Malachi battles the unseen, and is an unacknowledged hero to the most vulnerable. Most of the population have no idea what is really happening beneath the surface of the world in which they live.

In this collection of adventures, Malachi McKellan and Simon Tull wage war against the most insidious elements of the paranormal. In *The Three*, Malachi and Simon come to the aid of a young woman being victimized by a group of dark witches. An old apartment building is the scene of an unimaginable battle against monstrous forces in *The Lost Soul*. Malachi and Simon find themselves strategizing against a psychic vampire in *Obsession*, and *The Hotel* turns back time to the 1980s where Malachi confronts a demonic spirit. In *Between*, a past life is revisited as Malachi attempts to rescue a beloved sister from committing her existence to vengeance, and *The Wedding* takes a personal turn when Malachi must confront painful truths while endeavoring to protect his niece from a potentially devastating union.

Travel into the breach with a pair of paranormal warriors who choose to confront overwhelming forces on a battlefield unsuspected by most.

Gravier's Bookshop
A New Orleans Paranormal Mystery (#1)
6 x 9 Softcover & Hardcover 172 pages
ISBN 978-1-61342-288-5
ISBN (Hardcover) 978-1-61342-411-7

Max Gravier had no intention of becoming a recluse, but after his wife's death it seems his life is heading in that direction. He spends his time running Gravier's Bookshop on Magazine Street and occasionally on the quiet helps the police solve a crime with his psychic sensitivities. That is until he answers

Caroline Breslin's call, a cry for help out of his dreams that draws him into a fierce battle for a young woman's soul.

In this first installment of The New Orleans Paranormal Mystery series, Caroline Breslin, an amazingly gifted empath, is determined to strike out on her own and has moved out from the protection of her family home. All is going extremely well until, of course, she comes under siege from a devastating supernatural attack. The last thing Caroline wants is to run back to her family for help, even though she is painfully in over her head. What she really needs is a knight in shining armor — or maybe just that guy that keeps haunting her dreams.

Join them and the whole Breslin family psychic clan in this first installment of The New Orleans Paranormal Mystery Series where you'll travel into a new world just a few steps into the turbulent realm of the unseen.

The Hotel Mandolin
A New Orleans Paranormal Mystery (#2)
6 x 9 Softcover & Hardcover 146 pages
ISBN 978-1-61342-290-8
ISBN (Hardcover) 978-1-61342-412-4

Peril is wrapped up in the most enticing of disguises in *The Hotel Mandolin*, the second installment of The New Orleans Paranormal Mystery series. It's opulent, classic, and one of the most renowned hotels nestled deep in New Orleans' famous business district, but something is amiss at The Hotel Mandolin.

PI Peter Norfleet is calling out the big guns to help him investigate a recent suicide at the famous establishment — his good friend Max Gravier, a formidable psychic, and his girlfriend, Caroline Breslin, a talented empath. But none of them can seem to scratch the surface of this puzzle, no one except Cassie Breslin, Caroline's clairvoyant mother, who has somehow tapped into an unexpected connection with a tragic ghost from the turn of the century. And the more she uncovers, the more dangerous and malevolent the mystery becomes

The House at Pritchard Place
A New Orleans Paranormal Mystery (#3)
6 x 9 Softcover & Hardcover 138 pages
ISBN 978-1-61342-292-2
ISBN (Hardcover) 978-1-61342-413-1

Nothing is really wrong with the old Warrick House on Dante St. except that there most certainly is. Nothing is exactly wrong with its new mysterious owner except that Elise is sure that something doesn't add up. It isn't obvious, but sometimes the most dangerous things aren't.

In the third installment of The New Orleans Paranormal Mystery series, with the help of her very psychic sister and her children, the Breslin clan, Elise Ashford is about to embark on a wild rescue mission straight into another dimension that will land her squarely somewhere she doesn't expect, right back into her past. She'll land full circle; in a childhood home whose memory still haunts her to this day -- *The House at Pritchard Place.*

Treading on Borrowed Time
6 x 9 Softcover & Hardcover 223 pages
ISBN 978-1-61342-214-4
ISBN (Hardcover) ISBN (Hardcover) 978-1-61342-436-0

For Julia Moreau, life seems complicated. Emerging from a failed marriage and managing a lifetime of diabetes, she lives alone in her childhood home where she communicates with the spirit of her Great Aunt Lilia. But Julia doesn't have a clue what complicated is until she is thrust into being the key chess piece in a match between two powerful men of extraordinary abilities on the wild hunt for a mystical creature hidden in the heart of New Orleans' French Quarter. Will Julia lose her soul to the karma of a devastating past life or her heart to the love of a man driven by dark forces? What is clear is that whichever way she turns she is *Treading on Borrowed Time*.

Sanctuary of Echoes
6 x 9 Softcover & Hardcover 371 pages
ISBN 978-1-61342-211-3
ISBN (Hardcover) 978-1-61342-409-4

Ghosts unacknowledged do not sleep.

Corey Knight has resigned herself to a quiet, reclusive life spent living out the rest of her days in her childhood home on the fringes of New Orleans' French Quarter. But the unexpected specter of her deceased father plunges her into a mad quest for a missing supernatural weapon unearthed long ago. And unfortunately, her only ally is a lost love she once betrayed.

Iain Shaw returns to New Orleans, a city he abandoned a decade before while fleeing a devastating past. Here, he is forced to confront it again in the visage of the woman he once adored - one that he is now determined to get back at any cost.

Follow them both in a wild paranormal tale of discovery and redemption as they confront and unearth the echoes of a buried and unyielding truth that once tore them irreparably apart.

A Quiet Moment
6 x 9 Softcover & Hardcover 273 pages
ISBN 978-1-61342-326-4
ISBN (Hardcover) 978-1-61342-435-3

Jacob Wyss is caught in a rut, in fact on the verge of being engulfed by it. After an excruciating and disillusioning divorce, his life as an artist in a sleepy-college town at the foot of the Appalachian Mountains has become quiet, routine, and maddening in its predictability. One wintry day, his deep restlessness drives him out in precarious conditions to a largely empty bookstore nearly devoid of another living soul, nearly.

Aimee Marston isn't like everyone else. On the surface, she lives a sedate life working as a feature writer for a small local newspaper in addition to several other editorial jobs to help make ends meet. But just beneath, her existence is largely not her own. She is a sensitive, an empathetic psychic, guided by her calling to use her gifts to help others. Unfortunately, as a result, her secretiveness has made her defensive, protective of herself, and prevented her from having much of a life.

A psychic call for help sends Aimee out on a freezing January morning where her destiny and Jacob's collide sending both their lives spiraling onto an unexpected and often disturbing track. Two lonely souls connect, not by accident, but by design.

Theirs is the intersection of two spiritual paths, two lovers who must struggle to overcome the phantoms of a past life, as well as the challenges of their own inner demons to carve out an extraordinary future together.

A Ghost of a Chance
6 x 9 Softcover & Hardcover 230 pages
ISBN 978-1-61342-162-8
ISBN (Hardcover) 978-1-61342-440-7

You never know what's coming next.

Jack Brennan, an ambitious high-powered attorney, dies. But that's not the end, rather only the beginning. He finds himself constrained to an inexplicable afterlife as an earth-bound spirit trapped in an old Virginia farmhouse. His only companion is a very much living, reclusive writer of campy vampire novels. The maddening problem is that Hallie does not know he is there, nor that he is somewhat reluctantly falling in love with her.

Hallie Barkly is recovering from a painful and disillusioning divorce. Out of the ashes of her former life, she has managed to somehow forge a career and exorcise her demons by writing under the pseudonym of Sebastian Winters. Slowly, she is awakening to the fact that she is not alone.

Their lives intersect, and two unconventional lovers are brought together under insurmountable circumstances. Together they must battle an unseen force hell-bent on possessing Hallie's life and bridge death itself to make possible what cannot be — to find a chance.

Dragonflies - Journeys into the Paranormal
6 x 9 Softcover & Hardcover 176 pages
ISBN 978-1-88756-072-6
ISBN (Hardcover) 979-8-32548-418-6

In every form of creation, there is a blueprint for living, for experience, for interpretation. In flight, they can twist, turn, alter direction, pause in midair, and even fly backward. The dragonfly is the master of adaptability. They are a living prism, refracting light, and color, seemingly shifting their essence.

The lesson the dragonfly gives is that life is never what it appears to be.

In "The Wizard," as a novice practitioner of magic, Aurora Finn finds herself battling against the illusions of a powerful wizard intent on separating her from the world she knows. "The Sojourners" is a gentle story of a mother and daughter whose tenancy in an old Virginia farmhouse uncovers the trials and sorrows of its former occupants. A bookstore clerk gets an extraordinary customer on Halloween night in "Late One Night at Berstrums Books." In "The Tear," a woman coping with her fatal illness unknowingly begins a track on a mystical journey that will entirely restructure her vision of the world.

These stories follow the path of the dragonfly imbued with the momentum and energy of change, taking a winding and treacherous journey that ultimately leads to truth buried beneath perception.

Breaking Through the Pale
6 x 9 Softcover 134 pages
ISBN 978-1-88756-045-0

Journey with metaphysical author Evelyn Klebert into a collection of short stories that travel beyond the pale into the unpredictable realm of the paranormal.

In "A Grey Mourning," a disillusioned man encounters a mysterious being on the foggy streets of New Orleans. "Contact" is a tale of automatic writing, when a young artist establishes communication with a spirit guide, and the victim of a car crash unravels the true nature of her existence in "Dancing on the Threshold." The final tale is called "Isolation," in which a confused and disoriented woman finds herself in an old, quaint house where she must piece together the mystical implications surrounding her predicament.

Explanations
6 x 9 Softcover 82 pages
ISBN 978-1-93493-515-6

In this, her second poetry collection, Evelyn Klebert takes us down the intricate path of a personal journey. Life with its particular struggles, pitfalls, and ultimately triumphs clearly begins to mirror a universal path, the quest for answers that we all ultimately pursue. In this reflective, esoteric collection we can all explore and seek some of life's elemental mysteries and hopefully when all is said and done emerge with some *Explanations*.

The Witches' Own
6 x 9 Softcover & Hardcover 140 pages
ISBN 978-1-61342-058-4
ISBN (Hardcover) 978-1-61342-428-5

On the surface things seem quiet and serene in the pictur-esque coastal village of Kilmarnock, Virginia. But something unseen roams its lush forests as the past and present collide and the unthinkable begins to wreak its vengeance. Young Lucy Bonner is executed for witchcraft in the town's distant and bru-tal past. Her death triggers an unholy chain of events which grasp at the restless heart of novelist Peter McQuade, spurring him towards a quest to uncover the dark and terrifying truth.

The Left Palm
And Other Halloween Tales of the Supernatural
6 x 9 Softcover 117 pages
ISBN 978-1-93493-556-9

Halloween is the time of year when that veil between worlds is thinned, and you can just catch a quick glimpse into the realm of the unknowable. In this collection of short stories, Evelyn Klebert takes you to a place where ordinary life splinters into the sphere of the paranormal.

The journey begins with one woman's unstoppable quest for vengeance against a supernatural creature in "Wolves" and continues in an old historical graveyard where a horrifying dis-covery is uncovered in "Emma Fallon." In "The Soul Shredder," a psychiatrist's unusual patient opens his eyes to a disturbing new view of reality, while in "Wildflowers," a woman strikes up a supernatural friendship with impossible implications. And in

"The Left Palm," a fortuneteller in the French Quarter receives a most unexpected and terrifying customer.

The Broken Vow
Vol. I of The Clandestine Exploits of a Werewolf
6 x 9 Softcover & Hardcover 204 pages
ISBN 978-1-61342-133-8
ISBN (Hardcover) 978-1-61342-420-9

In the heart of every man there is a history. In the heart of every monster there is a story. In this first installment of *The Clandestine Exploits of a Werewolf*, Ethan Garraint is on a vendetta that begins in the heart of the Pyrenees with the fall of Montségur and leads him to the streets of New Orleans nearly five hundred years later. But the person he chases isn't really a man anymore and Ethan has been a werewolf for almost a millennium. With the aid of a gifted seer, he is on a blood hunt that will culminate in a journey that crosses the line between heaven and earth and ends somewhere in between.

Considerations
6 x 9 Softcover 68 pages
ISBN 978-1-88756-062-7

Sometimes the struggle to understand the meaning and complexities of living comes down to a single moment of introspection or a fleeting yet meaningful reflection. This collection of poetry by Evelyn Klebert takes you down a winding path of self-discovery where the resolution may not always be absolute, but the journey is indeed unforgettable. It a wide and varied map of inspired poetry for your examination and consideration.

Appointment with the Unknown
The Hotel Stories
6 x 9 Softcover & Hardcover 155 pages
ISBN 978-1-61342-360-8
ISBN (Hardcover) 978-1-61342-421-6

A hotel, for most, represents a normal place, a predictable realm of commonality. One might even go as far to say a safe space, the reliable where nothing particularly unusual is expected to happen. Or is it? Dimensional traveling, spirit guides, mystical storms, and soul mates separated by time are only a few elements dotting this supernatural landscape. Drop into a collection of romantic paranormal stories where that place of commonality is only the threshold, the jumping-off point, for extraordinary adventures into the unknown.

Visit Evelyn's website at:
www.evelynklebert.com

Cornerstone Book Publishers
www.cornerstonepublishers.com